Ava

Perfect Match Series

by

Denise Devine

True happiness is finding
your PERFECT MatcH!

Denise Devine

Ava

Perfect Match Series

Copyright 2018 by Denise Devine

www.deniseannettedevine.com

ISBN: 978-1-943124-07-7

Published in the United States of America

Edited by L.F. Nies and J. Dalton

Cover Design by Raine English

www.ElusiveDreamsDesigns.com

Introduction

You're cordially invited to spend an all-expenses-paid week-long trip to the island of your choice, courtesy of Perfect Match Online Dating and Travel Agency.

Grab your beach umbrella and prepare for six weeks of romance and fun in the sun with a brand-new series brought to you by *USA Today* bestselling authors...

Perfect Match!

Six exciting, sweet novellas linked by a unifying theme. You'll want to read each one!

PERFECT MATCH SERIES (AVA)

Six women receive invitations from Dawson Yates, owner of Perfect Match, a brand-new online matchmaking travel agency for a free week-long vacation to the island of her choice. As part of an extensive promotional campaign, Dawson expects to make six perfect matches that he can use to champion his business. The women expect to meet the men of their dreams. What none of them anticipates is the chaos that ensues when six couples who were strangers before agreeing to spend the week together discover that love is a lot more complicated than a match made by computer algorithms.

Join Bree, Marni, Molly, Jade, Ava, and Maeve as they embark on a once-in-a-lifetime vacation in the pursuit of love.

This is Ava's story...

It sounds too good to be true...

The invitation from "Perfect Match" offers Ava Godfrey an all-expense-paid week on Enchanted Island with the man of her dreams. Seven days of Caribbean sunshine, tropical beaches and candlelight dinners sounds like heaven. The only catch—she can't meet her Prince Charming until she arrives on the island. The scenario sounds risky, yet she finds the prospect intriguing. Will she find her "perfect match" or will she encounter the perfect scam?

They send him to deal with the diva...

Jeffrey Thomas has a job to do—cancel Ava Godfrey's contract. She's cost his boss a small fortune by turning down not one, but two matches sent to Enchanted Island by the agency. He's determined to cut her loose until he meets the spunky, fun-loving redhead and is irrevocably attracted to her. Though he's temped

2

to stay on the island and find out if she's his perfect match, his priority is to persuade her to go home. But when Ava's purse is stolen along with her identity, Jeff's only concern is helping her recover what she lost. Will he lose his heart to her in the process?

Meet the women of Perfect Match!

BREE (Raine English)

MARNI (Aileen Fish)

MOLLY (Julie Jarnagin)

JADE (Rachelle Ayala)

AVA (Denise Devine)

MAEVE (Josie Riviera)

Prologue

Ava's Perfect Match Dating Profile...

A Minnesota Girl – Age 31

Like everyone else, I've had my heart broken in the past, but I find it difficult to believe in the power of love.

Do you have what it takes to prove me wrong?

I'm looking for someone who is honest and genuine, a man who would accept me for who I am and bring out my true self—a crazy, fun-loving girl with an adventurous heart. If you really exist, you're one in a million.

And you just might be the one for me.

Chapter One

May 20th - West Palm Beach, Florida

The Perfect Gift

AVA GODFREY SAT in the plush seat of her rental car in the parking lot at the Silver Dolphin Restaurant, yawning loudly. She'd come all the way from Minneapolis to attend her best friend's baby shower and the last thing she needed was to be so tired she couldn't enjoy the party. She'd planned to catch a much-needed nap during her flight, but the plane had hit turbulence en route to the Palm Beach airport, leaving her white-knuckled and on the edge of her seat the entire trip. Once she'd arrived, the first thing she did was purchase a Starbucks Venti-sized cup of French Roast. It had helped somewhat, but the caffeine had left her more jittery than alert.

Darn, she thought as she flipped down her visor and focused on the woman staring back at her. *The best makeup in the world isn't going to conceal my state of mind.*

The mirror never lied. Her hazel eyes, underscored with dark circles against her pale skin showed fatigue, but also revealed the sad, faraway look she hadn't been able to shake since her divorce. Though she'd taken positive steps to move on, the mess she'd made of her life by marrying the wrong man still overshadowed the gregarious, fun-loving girl she used to be. Mistakes were easy to make. Starting over was not.

"Straighten up, honey," she said aloud as she searched her purse for a breath mint. "This is not the time to get sidetracked over what's wrong with *your* life. You have to show up with a smile on your face and a spring in your step so Lisa thinks you're doing great."

Her phone rang. With a sigh, she picked it off the seat and swiped the screen. The ID displayed *Lisa Kaye-Wells.* "Hi, Lisa," she said in a rush.

"Ava, where *are* you?" Music, chatter and laughter echoed in the background. "You're supposed to be here by now." Though their lives had changed since their days of rooming together at college, their differences hadn't. Lisa still proved to be the punctual one. Ava was still always rushing in at the last minute.

"I'm in the parking lot. See you in five minutes.

Bye." She touched up her peach lipstick and shut off the car. Grabbing her purse, her phone and her baby gift, Ava braced herself against the drizzling Florida afternoon as she locked her car then sprinted across the parking lot to the restaurant.

She arrived at the front door at the same time as a well-dressed couple in their mid-forties. The man, tall and slim with graying dark hair, stood aside and opened the door for her. "Thank you," she said as she entered the two-story building made of steel and glass overlooking the Atlantic Ocean. She hurried past the gift shop to the host stand and approached a young woman with burgundy hair standing behind a black podium arranging a stack of menus. "Hello, I'm looking for the Wells reception."

The woman pointed toward the stairs. "It's in the upper level."

"Thank you." Squaring her shoulders, Ava trudged up the wide, open stairway to a large room with floor-to-ceiling windows facing the ocean. Round tables covered with white linen and adorned with small vases of fresh pink, white and yellow flowers were scattered about the room. A buffet filled with assorted hot and cold appetizers, fruit, punch and desserts stretched the length of an entire wall. Lisa stood near the gift table, wearing a floor-length, yellow dress with an empire waist, emphasizing her round "baby bump." Her long dark hair hung down her back in soft, spiral curls.

"Ava," she cried as she held out her arms for a hug, "I'm so glad you're here. We haven't seen each other in ages!"

The last year had gone by fast. Ava placed her gift on the table, vowing to herself not to let another year go by before they saw each other again.

They exchanged hugs. "How are you? You look terrific," Ava exclaimed as they pulled apart. "Motherhood really agrees with you."

"How have *you* been?" Lisa asked, turning the focus back on her. "Shawn and I have talked about flying up to Minnesota to see you, but the hotel we own booked solid every week and it's impossible to get away. He wanted to be here today, but we had back-to-back weddings scheduled this weekend so he couldn't leave the island."

Lisa grew up in West Palm Beach, but she and Shawn Wells, her husband of one year, presently owned and operated a historic hotel on Enchanted Island, located about fifty miles off the southern tip of Florida.

The couple had met there several years earlier, when Lisa worked in her Aunt Elsie's B&B and Shawn had managed his family's hotel. They'd surprised everyone when they acquired the rundown Morganville Hotel and began restoring it, turning it into a popular destination in the East Caribbean. Since then, Lisa and Shawn had married and were starting their family.

"I'm doing fine," Ava said with a smile.

"Are you sure?" Lisa's brows furrowed. "I can't help worrying about you. This past year has been so difficult—"

"Hey, you have enough to worry about right here," Ava said as she patted Lisa's rounded tummy. "I can't wait to see your little mini-me when she makes her debut into the world!"

The couple that had followed Ava into the building approached them, greeting Lisa and diverting her attention. Realizing Lisa needed to attend to her other guests, Ava glanced around the room looking for the bar. She'd decided to get a glass of Cabernet and find somewhere to sit down, but before she could wander away, Lisa grabbed her by the arm and introduced her to Shawn's brother and sister-in-law, Ian and Belinda Wells.

"Come and sit with me later when you get a few minutes," Ava said as more people arrived and crowded around Lisa. "In the meantime, I'm going to have a couple of those deep-fried wontons from the buffet and a glass of wine."

"You rat," Lisa whispered with an envious smile. "I haven't had any booze or junk food for six months. Have a glass for me, too."

"I will!" Ava laughed. "Don't worry, it won't be long before you'll be able to eat whatever you want."

Many of Lisa's friends from her online book club were there. Ava stood in line at the bar with one of the women. "You're Tara, right?" She smiled at the pretty brunette as she waited for the bartender to pour her a glass of wine. "I remember you from Lisa's wedding."

"I remember you, too," Tara replied. "You're Ava—Lisa's college friend from Minnesota. Are you here by yourself? Come and sit with us." She pointed toward a large round table filled with five vivacious women. "All of the out-of-towners have gathered together."

"All right," Ava said, curious about the women Lisa had befriended online. After they received their drinks, she accompanied Tara to the table and Tara introduced her to the group, naming them from left to right—Amy, Clair, Meg, Jenny and Hope.

For the next hour, she sat and sipped her wine while listening to amusing stories about the books they'd read and their retreat on Enchanted Island where all twelve members of the group had met for the first time. Each woman had tossed a bottle containing a message to her *dream hero* into the bay. Though Ava refrained from joining in the conversation, she truly enjoyed hearing about this pretty island that everyone seemed to love so much. Something in her heart stirred, creating in her a yearning to visit Lisa and Shawn on Enchanted Island once their little girl, Emma, was born.

"Oh, my gosh, Ava. This is the perfect gift! Thank you!"

Lisa stood at the gift table pulling out the contents of a large, handmade diaper bag filled with a girl's layette. She waved for Ava to join her. "Where did you find such precious little outfits?"

"My Aunt Ruth made them and the bag, too. Did you see the newborn diapers?"

"Oh, look at this," Lisa said as she pulled out a box filled with several pairs of miniature fleece slipper-socks and a white, crocheted baptism set. There were Onesies, sleepers, receiving blankets, bibs and changing pads. At the bottom of the bag, Lisa found two dozen tiny diapers made with soft flannel in pastel colors. A chorus of oohs and ahhs came from women in the room as Lisa held up each different item. She carefully packed all of the pieces back into the bag and set it aside.

"Now," she said to Ava, "I have something for you." Lifting the floor-length tablecloth, she reached under the table where she'd stored her belongings and pulled out an envelope from her purse. "Here," she said as she straightened and offered it to Ava. "This is something special just *for you*."

"For me?" Ava gingerly accepted the white square envelope. "What is it?"

Lisa's eyes widened with anticipation. "Well, open it and you'll find out!"

Inside, Ava discovered an invitation. She pulled out the embossed card and stared at it—speechless—as she read the words.

> *You're cordially invited to spend an all-expenses-paid, week-long trip to the island of your choice, courtesy of Perfect Match Online Dating and Travel Agency.*

"What is this?" Ava laughed, thinking it was a joke of some kind that Lisa had received and wanted to show her. "A clever new way to hook people into a timeshare presentation?"

Lisa blinked, taken back. "No, it's nothing like that! Look at it again."

Ava scanned the invitation a second time. Was it real, after all? "Are you saying this invitation is for me personally?" Lisa nodded. "Why me? Why aren't you offering this to one of your book club friends?" She tried to give it back, but Lisa refused.

Lisa pushed her hand away. "Don't you see, this is just what you need—seven days on a beautiful island with nothing to do but kick back and enjoy yourself!"

Ava frowned. "What would I do on a tropical island by myself?"

"You're not going to be alone." Lisa laughed, sounding as though she thought Ava was kidding again. "The agency will select the perfect match for you."

The wha—what?

"I hope you didn't pay a lot of money for this," Ava replied as she smacked the invitation on the table, "because you're not setting me up with a total stranger for a solid week. What, are you crazy? Allowing an agency to select my *perfect match* is the most ridiculous, hair-brained scheme I've ever heard of. I mean, that stuff is for adventurous twenty-year-olds with romantic dreams. It's not practical for a thirty-one-year-old-woman who has been previously married. And failed at it. The last thing I need is to be stuck out in the middle of nowhere with a blind date for seven days." She watched Lisa's smile fade and instantly regretted her hasty refusal. "I'm sorry. I know you mean well, Lisa, but this is definitely not my style." She pointed toward the table of Lisa's friends. The women were watching them intently, causing her to wonder if they were secretly in on this, too. "Really, I think you should give it to one of them."

Lisa shook her head. "They already have invitations of their own. Amy's fiancé, Dawson Yates, owns the agency and he gave each member of the book club a complimentary invitation to pass along to the person of her choice."

Oops... Ava's cheeks flamed with embarrassment. Amy had heard every word she'd said.

Lisa picked up the invitation and put it back into Ava's hand. "My choice is *you.*"

"But...but, I'm not ready to start dating yet."

Lisa smiled patiently. "Take it from me, Ava. No one *ever is* after a bad break up. You need to take a chance, step outside your comfort zone and meet someone new."

Stunned by her best friend's persistence, Ava didn't know what else to say. Suddenly, all of the women in the book club stood up and walked over to them. Amy Sheridan, the one with curly, dark brown hair and green eyes, stepped forward.

"I understand your apprehension," Amy said in a soft tone, "but my fiancé's agency is top-notch and that means he's careful about the matches he coordinates. Once you establish a profile online, a Perfect Match Specialist will match you with someone who shares common interests with you." Her eyes twinkled as she placed her hand on Ava's arm. "If you accept the invitation, you only have one obligation to Perfect Match. You must stay the entire week. That's it. Just have a fun-filled vacation with your match, taking in the sun and enjoying the beauty of your destination. I can assure you with full confidence that your satisfaction is Dawson's utmost concern."

"What's the catch?" Ava folded her arms. "What does your fiancé want in return for giving me this free offer?"

Amy's expression changed from soft to serious.

"You'll be given a survey at the end of your week to grade your satisfaction on how well the agency handled setting up your trip—and your match. Plus, you may be asked to participate in a promotional video. I have no doubt that you'll be very happy with *all* of the arrangements."

"Other than the seven-day stipulation, the survey and the promotional video, there are no strings attached?"

Amy shook her head. "None."

Lisa's soft jade eyes took on a pleading look. "Come on, Ava, accept the invitation. You've been through so much this past year. You deserve a break. Do this for yourself, okay?"

"I've never even browsed a dating site, much less one that sends you to an exotic location to meet your so-called perfect match," Ava said, running out of objections. "Where would I go?"

Lisa held up her palms. "Well, that's a no-brainer. Isn't it?"

"Enchanted Island!" Lisa's friends responded in a chorus then they burst out laughing.

Lisa laughed so hard she contracted a pain in her side and had to lean with one palm on the table. "This is perfect," she said, clutching her side. "I'm due at the end of August. Book your trip for the last week and be with me when the baby is born!"

The chance to be present when Lisa had her baby sounded tempting, but...

Maybe a trip some place far away from my problems in Minnesota is the prescription I need to pull myself together and start thinking about my future. Spending quality time with my best friend wouldn't hurt, either. Maybe I should accept the invitation and spend my week in Enchanted Island when Lisa is due. It sounds like a wonderful place and frankly, my life is so dull...

But—finding her perfect match in a computer database through an online dating system? The thought made her almost laugh out loud.

Chapter Two

Wednesday, September 2nd – Minneapolis, Minnesota

The Perfect Plan

JEFFREY THOMAS SAT in his home office at his computer, waiting apprehensively for his meeting to begin. His boss, Dawson Yates, had hurriedly set it up online, but Jeff had no idea what Dawson wanted to discuss. He'd been with Perfect Match Online Dating and Travel Agency as a Perfect Match Specialist since the company started up one year ago. His basic duties included, but were not limited to, introducing clients to their perfect matches and working with each couple to plan every detail of their "perfect" getaway where they would physically meet for the first time. The company's main office was located in South Carolina, but since the Specialists performed most of their work online, Dawson had assembled a team of the best people from around the country.

Suddenly Dawson's face flashed on the screen—a man in his mid-thirties with short black hair, a golden tan and an unmistakable air of confidence. "Good morning, J. T. How's the weather up there in Minnesota? Is it snowing yet?"

"Good morning, Dawson." Jeff sat up straight, anxious to get through the niceties and tackle the main topic of this meeting. For some reason, Dawson always referred to him as J.T. rather than his actual name. He didn't mind, but he often wondered if Dawson used initials for all of his other employees, too. "No, it's actually been pretty nice all week. The leaves are starting to reach their peak of fall color."

"We're hoping to dodge the hurricane blowing through the northern half of Florida right now," Dawson said. "It's been downgraded to a tropical storm and it's veering toward the Atlantic as we speak, but if it builds up steam out there and steers back toward the coast, we could get hit pretty hard."

No thanks, Jeff thought. *I'll take a good old-fashioned snowstorm any day over that business.*

"One of the reasons we're meeting today, Jeff," Dawson said in a businesslike tone as he changed the subject, "is to talk about some changes taking place in the company."

Jeff froze, blindsided by Dawson's statement. *Is he going to fire me?* It sounded like an introduction to bad news...

"Those free memberships we gave out last spring have generated a lot of referrals and positive reviews. Business is growing at a faster rate than I had anticipated," Dawson continued. "A large percentage of our new business is coming from the Midwest so I've decided to set up a regional office in Minneapolis. I'd like you to take the reins of that project and start looking for suitable space to lease. Since you have prior project management experience and your references have nothing but good things to say about you, I'm confident you'll live up to the task."

Jeff blinked, surprised by Dawson's expansion plans, but excited over the announcement of a regional office. "I'll be happy to do that," he said, though his voice sounded preoccupied. His mind was already jumping ahead to contacting a leasing agent, finding a contractor to handle the leasehold improvements, purchasing furniture and equipment...

"Great, then it's settled. You're the project manager and you'll handle the entire process. We'll meet once a week online or as often as you need to discuss your progress."

"When do you want me to start looking for space? Will I be working alone or will the new office manager be included in the development planning, too?"

"Well, that depends, J.T. Would you like to ratchet things up another level?"

"Meaning..."

Dawson smiled. "You're my preferred choice for the regional manager position, too. That is, if you want the job."

Jeff gave a silent cheer. In less than five minutes, his career had taken a major turn. He hadn't expected it, but he didn't need time to think about it, either. "Yes, I do!"

"All right," Dawson said. "If the weather holds up, I'm having a retreat this weekend at my home here in South Carolina for my new managers. I know it's last minute, but I'd like you to attend. You'd be flying in on Thursday night. Are you available?"

"Absolutely," Jeff said eagerly. "I'm looking forward to it."

"Good. In the meantime, I have another small job

for you. I'd do it myself, but I'm busy putting together all of my materials for the retreat."

Something in the way Dawson's brows furrowed and his voice suddenly dropped an octave gave Jeff pause. "Is this a serious matter?"

Dawson's jaw visibly clenched. "It has the potential to be if it's not handled right."

Jeff stared hard at the face on the screen. "Are you asking me to fire someone?"

Dawson ran his hand through his thick, dark hair, showing a level of anxiety Jeff had never seen before. "In a way, yes, but it's more delicate than that."

For a moment, both sat like statues, absorbing the weight of his words. Dawson broke the silence with a sigh.

"Okay, so it's like this—we have a particularly sensitive situation with a client who accepted a complimentary certificate from one of Amy's friends." Dawson tapped his pen on the desk, obviously working off tension. "We sent the client to Enchanted Island to meet her match and she rejected him before the week was out. She called me; very upset, claiming I'd mismatched her." He shook his head. "So, I pulled up her list of matches and set her up with the next client on her list. Surprisingly, the guy was able to drop everything and fly down there on a day's notice." Dawson drew in a deep breath and squared his shoulders. "It took her less time than that to tell him to take a hike."

Jeff winced, knowing what came next, but he had to ask anyway. "So, what do you want me to do?"

"Because it's a friend of one of the members of Amy's book club, this has to be handled face to face. I don't want to upset Amy over this so I want you to fly to Enchanted Island and personally talk to the woman. Tell her she's not eligible for any more free matches because the contract has been fulfilled—on our part, anyway. Offer her a complimentary voucher for a vacation somewhere else at a later date. It's simply a goodwill gesture on our part. We didn't mismatch her."

"If she filled out her profile honestly, there's no way we could have given her the wrong match either time," Jeff argued. "Our system has been scientifically proven to be ninety-nine percent effective."

Dawson shrugged. "You and I know that, but there's no reasoning with this woman. She's convinced it's our mistake and that's that. She's expecting me to get back to her soon, so I'd like you to fly down there right away. Take care of the situation and then come straight to the retreat."

That meant he had to call off his plans for tonight. A guy only had a birthday once a year and this year, he'd planned to celebrate turning thirty-five at the ballpark drinking beer and eating pizza with the guys. Normally, it wouldn't have been a problem rescheduling his night out, but it had taken no less than a small miracle to get six tickets to this event. The Minnesota Twins were one game away from clinching the American League Central Division Championship and he'd been looking forward to viewing that game from a lower deck seat at Target Field. Nevertheless, Dawson's situation was more important and though Jeff hated to cancel his plans, he had plenty of friends who would gladly buy the ticket from him.

Yesterday, the hurricane had forced the Miami airport to temporarily close, but if it was back into full operation today, he could try to get a red-eye flight to Miami tonight and a hopper flight to Enchanted Island tomorrow morning. Take a day to handle his business and make it to Dawson's place in South Carolina in time for the retreat.

But he needed to know one more thing.

"Who am I meeting with? What's the woman's

name?"

"You might remember her profile. Her name is Ava Godfrey. She's the last client in our beta group to use her complimentary week."

His mind went into a tailspin. *She was the one? Oh-oh...*

Yeah, he remembered her. He'd seen her profile and her photo a few times in the course of his work. How could he forget that gorgeous redhead? She had long, thick hair and prominent hazel eyes that could mesmerize you if you stared at her picture too long. He never dwelled on client profiles, but in her case, he found it difficult *not* to stare. Dawson had personally contacted all of the women who'd received complimentary invitations by the book club members, including Ms. Godfrey's match. Jeff thought he'd forgotten about her, but the moment Dawson mentioned her, his curiosity returned, stronger than ever.

Fortunately, he didn't intend to be on Enchanted Island long enough to risk falling under her spell...

****

All went according to plan and by early afternoon the next day, Jeff checked into his room at the Dolphin

Bay Resort on Enchanted Island. He changed into shorts and a short-sleeved shirt, had lunch in the Starfish Cafe and went into the lobby, deciding to quit delaying the inevitable. He needed to meet up with Ms. Godfrey and relay Dawson's instructions.

The trouble was, he didn't know where to find her. He'd called both her room and her cell phone and got her voicemail each time. Why would she not be answering her calls? Assuming she was somewhere in the resort complex enjoying the amenities, he set out to find her. He checked everywhere in the hotel, including inquiring with the receptionist at the spa and he'd finally concluded she must be on the beach. That, however, proved to be a daunting prospect in itself. Hundreds of guests clad in tropical beachwear populated the multiple pools, hot tubs and the beaches of Dolphin Bay. He checked out the pools and the pool bars then wandered toward the beach. After about twenty minutes of roaming through countless rows of people sunning themselves on the beach, he concluded he wouldn't find her and had decided to give up. That's when he saw her reading a book under an umbrella, lying on a chaise lounge in a sleek, white bathing suit, stretching out her long, shapely legs. Though she wore oversized sunglasses and a floppy, white hat, he had no trouble recognizing key features from her photo—the long, slender neck and those thick, coppery curls framing her rectangular face.

He strolled toward her, giving himself time to formulate the right words to say. She looked up from her novel and paused, staring straight at him. He didn't know why, but the closer he came to this beautiful woman, the more his nerves jangled. He stopped at the foot of her chair. "Hello, are you Ava Godfrey?" At her nod, he continued. "I'm Jeff Thomas from The Perfect Match Online Dating and Travel Agency. I'm here to—"

"I was expecting Dawson Yates," she said in a smooth, sultry voice and lowered her sunglasses, revealing prominent hazel eyes fringed with long, dark lashes. "He's the person who set up my matches and the last time I talked to him, he assured me he was *personally* going to handle this mess. Why did he send you?"

Most women didn't rattle him, but something about the fiery look in Ava Godfrey's eyes threw him off balance, turning him into a bumbling fool. The moment she spoke, sweat began to collect on the back of his neck. Because he'd had to make travel arrangements on the spur of the moment, he hadn't had time to get a haircut before coming to the island and he was paying for it now.

His thick, curly hair collected on the nape of his neck, causing him to heat up at a time when he needed to stay cool and calm. "Don't worry, Ms. Godfrey, I have the authority on Dawson's behalf to—"

"Good, then I assume that means you're prepared to get physical if necessary."

He almost swallowed his tongue. "*Wh-what?*"

She removed her sunglasses and slipped them inside her clear, vinyl beach bag. Her beautiful eyes flashed with anger. "Perfect Mismatch Number Two won't quit stalking me."

Chapter Three

Thursday, September 3rd - Enchanted Island

The Perfect Storm

THE TALL, BLOND man standing before her in khaki shorts and a blue Tommy Bahama shirt stared at her in disbelief. "*Who?*"

"Richard Santorio," Ava said, fuming. "The second match that Dawson Yates set up for me." She slid her legs over the side of the chaise and slipped on her sandals. "Some consolation *he* turned out to be. What are you going to do about him?" Ava stood up, tossing her romance novel into her beach bag. His speechlessness apparently meant he had no idea what she was talking about. "As I explained to Dawson, Richard's behavior has proved he is definitely *not* my perfect match, but he won't take no for an answer."

Jeff Thomas' stunned expression turned serious, his golden brows furrowing. "Did he threaten you? Is that why you're not answering your phone?"

She picked up her flowing white caftan and slipped it on. "No, but he keeps calling me and suddenly shows up when I least expect it, demanding I give him another chance. I put my phone on voicemail and I've stayed out of sight because I thought I could handle this matter myself, but I decided today that I wasn't going to avoid him any longer. If he confronts me again, I'll turn the matter over to the resort's security team."

"Just call me Jeff," he said to her as he scanned the crowded beach. "Is he around here now? I don't see him. If you know where he is, just point him out and I'll take care of the problem right away."

Richard Santorio was a well-built man, but Jeff Thomas stood taller and, judging by his solid, muscular chest and sculpted biceps, could probably hold his own. She hoped it wouldn't come to that, however.

"No, I don't see him in this crowd," she replied, glancing around. "That doesn't mean he's not here, though." She picked up her bag, ready to escape the heat and the bright sun. "To set the record straight, if you've come here to play mediator, I will not kiss and make up. I think it would be best if Richard went home and looked for another match."

"No, I'm not here to take sides or try to get you two back together. However, because Richard isn't abiding by the rules of the contract—which states that participants are expressly prohibited from harassing or stalking each other in the event one party terminates the match—I do need to know exactly what is going on." Jeff took one last look around, presumably searching for anyone who seemed out of place. "Why don't we get out of this heat and go someplace cooler where we can talk?"

"All right," Ava said and fell into step beside him. Hopefully, now she'd get this mess peaceably resolved. "I know of a quiet place where we can do just that and if Richard is presently stalking us, we'll confront him there when he shows up. Follow me."

She led him to a lush, tropical garden situated along the shady side of the resort with tall, overarching palms, chirping birds and colorful, fragrant flowers lining a curved stone path.

Jeff stopped next to a small, stone bench and motioned her to sit. "Please, tell me what's going on."

"From the beginning or just the part where Richard is concerned?"

Folding his arms, he leaned his back against a palm tree as though preparing to be there a while. "Why don't you begin where the trouble started?"

H-m-m-m... How about the day Lisa handed me the invitation and insisted I take a chance on finding my perfect match?

She sat on the bench and set her beach bag next to her. "Perfect Mismatch Number one: Henry Hamilton. Nice guy, handsome, the whole bit, but he was a workaholic who wouldn't quit looking at his watch. He spent more time staring at his wrist than communicating eye-to-eye with me. He never heard half of what I said. When I finally complained, Henry insisted he needed to check his email." She raised her hands into the air. "*Excuse me?* He was in a restaurant overlooking an unforgettable view of the moonlight glowing across the Caribbean with a woman who was supposed to be his *perfect match* and he couldn't quit *checking his email*?" She slipped off one sandal and let it drop to the ground, smacking the sand from the sole of her foot. "I definitely had a cause for complaint and I said so to Dawson Yates. Dawson apologized and set me up with Perfect Mismatch Number Two: Richard Santorio." She expelled a deep sigh. "Richard turned out to be even worse than Henry."

Jeff's skeptical frown suggested he regarded her story the self-centered ramblings of a diva. "I can understand one wrong match, but two? Why did you reject Santorio, if I may ask?"

She pulled off her other sandal and looked up. "He's too much like my ex-husband."

"Dawson matched you to both of the men based on your profiles. According to the information you provided, these men are exactly your type."

His insistence on Perfect Match's *perfect system* irritated her. "Then maybe I'm attracted to the wrong kind of man."

"And what kind is that..."

"A control freak—" She sprang from the bench, throwing her hands in the air. "Listen, Mr. Perfect Match Specialist, there's more to finding the right man and falling in love than just comparing data on a form!"

"You're right," he said. "The profile doesn't guarantee you'll gain trust or respect or live happily ever after with that person. Just the same, you have to start somewhere. You have to be willing to give, rather than take, if you want to build a strong foundation in a relationship."

If only...

His directness had touched a nerve. He obviously

didn't know it, but he'd nailed the problem she'd struggled with in her marriage almost from day one. Her ex-husband had cared about only one opinion and one person's needs—his own.

She'd become so invested in making her feelings known, she hadn't realized how close they stood to each other. Close enough to notice his eyes were as blue as the Caribbean sky. Close enough to breathe in his spicy cologne.

"In that case, I—I don't know if I'll ever find the right man. Truly unselfish men are few and far between."

"I'm sorry you feel that way," he said softly, taking her hand in his. The moment their palms touched, her pulse suddenly leaped. "Not all men are like that."

"Well, well, what do we have here?"

They pulled away as a tall, dark-haired man wearing flip-flops, jean shorts and a red tank top strode toward them.

"Richard," Ava said, barely holding back her exasperation, "I told you to leave me alone. What are you doing here?"

Chapter Four

Thursday, September 3rd

The Perfect Solution

RICHARD SANTORIO'S COFFEE-COLORED eyes flashed with anger as he stabbed the air with his finger. "I want to know who he is! Is this why you dumped me? You've found yourself a long-haired surfer dude? Or, did you plan all along to accept the free trip and meet your real boyfriend here?"

"Settle down, Santorio," Jeff said as he held up his palms in a gesture of peace. In the past, ex-boyfriends of women he'd dated had called him a variety of colorful names, but never that one. "I'm not her boyfriend or her 'surfer dude,' although I've caught a few waves in my time. I'm Jeff Thomas from Perfect Match Online Dating and Travel Agency."

He walked toward Richard and held out his palm to shake hands. Richard ignored it and instead gave him a threatening glare. "What do you want, reimbursement for all my expenses because *she* rejected her match? Well, forget it. I'm not paying for something I didn't get."

The way Santorio spat the word *get* as his gaze roamed over Ava's shapely body left no doubt in Jeff's mind what the man had expected. And why she'd quickly backed off.

Withdrawing his hand, Jeff smiled, disregarding the fact that Richard had just insulted him. "Actually, I'm here to give *you* something, both of you. Perfect Match is concerned about your satisfaction, so I've come on the company's behalf to give you each a voucher for another vacation. We've fulfilled our end of your contracts, but we realize this is an unusual circumstance and we don't want either of you to leave the island unhappy."

Any more than you already are...

"We're gifting you each a voucher for a seven-day stay in the continental U.S., the Caribbean or Mexico at any of our approved properties." Dawson hadn't said anything about giving a consolation gift to Santorio, but Jeff made a snap decision to award him one as well so he'd go away quietly and not cause any more public embarrassment to Ava or the agency. In Jeff's mind, the jerk actually deserved a right hook to the jaw for treating

Ava so disrespectfully, but he kept his cool. "The voucher is for a vacation, nothing more. If you decide to pursue another match through our online dating system, you'll have to pay for that travel yourself. I'll make arrangements today for both of you to use your return trip flight tickets home tomorrow. Do you have any questions?"

Ava turned to him. "May I use my voucher right away?"

"I'm afraid not," Jeff said. "You'll have to go through a Perfect Match Specialist to make your travel arrangements at least a month in advance of your trip, based on availability."

She looked crestfallen.

He didn't know why, but her disappointment tugged at his heart. "What's wrong?"

She shrugged. "It's just that I have a friend who lives on the island and I'd hoped I'd be here when she had her baby. She's overdue and expecting her daughter any day now."

"You can extend your stay here if you'd like, but it's at your own expense."

She shook her head. "I can't afford to stay here on

my own. The resorts on this island are beautiful, but the price tag for an all-inclusive night's lodging is phenomenal."

"Why don't you stay with your friend?"

"I know it sounds like the logical thing to do, but I can't stay with Lisa, either. She and her husband own the Morganville Hotel downtown and it's so popular, it's fully booked all the time. Besides, she's currently on bed rest and her mother is staying with her, taking care of her, so they don't have any room for me in their private suite. I'd just be in the way, anyway."

Jeff nodded sympathetically. "The flight back to Miami leaves tomorrow at noon. I'll make arrangements at the bell station for the three of us to take the hotel shuttle to the Morganville airport."

"Good enough," Richard said, sounding almost civil. "I'll be there." He turned and walked away, not bothering to say goodbye or thank Jeff for the consolatory gift.

"Good *riddance*," Ava whispered. She picked up her sandals, grabbed her bag and started walking toward the hotel.

"Since this is your last night at the resort, would

you like to meet later for cocktails and a farewell dinner? I can give you the flight information at that time as well." Jeff suddenly called after her. He hadn't planned that; the words just came out.

She turned back. "Thank you for the offer, but since I'm leaving tomorrow, I need to get packed and make some phone calls. I'll probably order room service instead."

She left him standing alone in the garden, wondering why her decision to spend her last night on the island alone disappointed him so much.

****

Friday, September 4th

The next morning, Jeff met Ava, Richard and a small group of additional departing guests at the bell station. He'd gone down earlier to request a printout of his bill and have a quick breakfast before grabbing his duffel bag and checking out of his room. As he walked out of the elevator with his duffel bag slung over his shoulder, the hotel's transport vehicle arrived, parking under the covered entrance.

"Good morning, everyone," Jeff said to the group as the glass doors whisked open and they all walked toward the small shuttle bus. The driver stood at the luggage compartment, loading passenger bags.

Ava wore a long summer dress in a shiny fabric of silvery gray with clusters of white, blue and peach flowers splashed across the garment. She'd pulled her long hair into a ponytail with wispy curls framing her face. Jeff stood in line behind her as she surrendered her suitcase to the driver and boarded the vehicle. She took a seat next to an elderly lady. Jeff took the seat across the aisle from her, securing a spot by the window. Richard took the only seat left, which was next to him.

He and Richard had nothing to say to each other during the half hour ride to the airport. When the bus pulled up in the drop-off lane behind another shuttle, Richard jumped out of his seat to be the first one off. Jeff allowed Ava and the elderly woman to exit first, following right behind them as they walked around the bus to claim their bags.

As they pulled their luggage toward the crosswalk that led to the terminal, Jeff glanced over his shoulder and noticed a scooter motoring slowly into the drop-off lane. The driver didn't seem to be looking for a place to park. Rather, it appeared to be veering straight toward them. The driver's odd behavior made him uneasy.

Vehicles were supposed to slow down in the lane and stop for people in the crosswalk. As it neared them, however, it sped up.

"Ava, watch out!"

Jeff grabbed Ava by the arm and pulled her out of harm's way, but not before the scooter driver reached out and snatched the handbag off her shoulder, nearly knocking her down in the process. It sped away.

"NO!" Ava let go of her suitcase and tried to chase after the thief. "He's got my purse! That man stole my purse!"

Jeff caught up to her and grabbed her by the arms. "You'll never catch him." He stopped, breathing heavily, the duffle still hanging from his shoulder. "He's gone."

"What am I going to do, Jeff?" Tears filled her eyes. "That man stole my identification, my credit card and my money. I can't get on the plane without it." She tossed her hands in the air in frustration. "I've got to get it back!"

Jeff churned with anger as the scooter raced away from the airport grounds and disappeared into the countryside. He didn't know what the procedure was here for reporting a crime, but he planned to find out.

"The first thing you're going to do," he said to her in a soft voice, "is calm down. We'll locate a police officer in the airport and find out what the procedure is for reporting the theft."

"I didn't think things could get any worse for me here, but I guess I was wrong," she said in a tearful voice. "Now, I'm stranded."

Not if I can help it...

One of the other passengers had retrieved her suitcase in the crosswalk and rolled it over to her, offering his sympathy on her loss. With a tearful nod, she thanked him and pulled her purple suitcase close, gripping the handle with white-knuckled hands.

"Come on," Jeff said, "let's find someone to assist us." He gently grabbed the handle of her suitcase in one hand, cupped her elbow with the other and escorted her to the terminal entrance.

An armed officer wearing a uniform of camouflage material exited through the glass doors with his K-9 "sniffer" dog as they approached. Jeff introduced himself and Ava to the man and explained their situation. The officer called for assistance on his radio and escorted them to the Airport Police Operations Center, a small office with an outside entrance to the terminal.

Within a few minutes, another officer arrived in an older model Jeep with the words POLICE painted on the door. The tall, lanky islander stepped out of the vehicle wearing royal blue trousers with a gold stripe and a deep yellow, short-sleeved shirt with epaulets. And blue Nike tennis shoes. "Good afternoon, I'm Sheriff Duane Hall," he said in a deep Caribbean accent, pronouncing his title "Sher-EEF" and his name "Dee-WAYNE. He approached them with a sober look on his face and his thumbs tucked inside his heavily equipped duty belt. "I understand you've had your bag stolen in a drive-by in-cee-dent."

"Yes, I did," Ava said. "It contained cash, my ID and my American Express card."

He rubbed his closely trimmed beard. "Did you get a good look at da thief? Can you describe him for me?"

She shook her head and dabbed at her eyes with a tissue.

The crime had happened so fast, Jeff had barely enough time to pull Ava out of the way much less get a good look at the assailant, but he did remember the man wore a maroon shirt, sunglasses and a black bill cap. He drove a faded green scooter.

Sheriff Hall had Ava sign the necessary forms and advised her to cancel her credit card.

"I had my phone in my purse. It's gone, too..."

Jeff patted his phone in his pocket. "You can use mine."

"We will send out a notice to local businesses with a description of da suspect, but I can't make any promee-says," Sheriff Hall declared and handed Ava his card. "In da meantime, call me if you think of anything else."

They thanked the sheriff and left the police station.

"I guess I'll give Lisa's mother a call and find out if I can stay with them until I get another credit card and a replacement ID," Ava said. "I'll sleep on the floor if I have to; I'm desperate."

Jeff held out his phone, but he stopped just short of giving it to her. "I've got a better idea. I'll call Dawson and tell him what happened. In view of the circumstances, I think I can convince him to allow you to use your voucher right now."

Ava's face brightened. "Thank you. I hope he agrees." She bit her lip. "I'm afraid I haven't been the nicest person where he is concerned and I wouldn't blame him if he turned me down flat."

Jeff promptly placed a call to Dawson and relayed the information.

Dawson agreed, as he had expected. "Are you going to hang around for a day or so, J.T.? You may need to ID the thief if they catch him."

Dawson's question caught him up short. He hadn't thought of that. "You're right. I need to take care of this."

"I'll leave it up to you," Dawson said. "Do whatever you think is best."

"If I stay, I won't make it to the retreat." Jeff stared at the ground, worried about missing his first managerial meeting and all the important information Dawson would be sharing, not to mention meeting his new peers. The other managers were due to arrive at Dawson's house today.

"Don't worry, I'll save copies of everything for you."

"Okay. I'll call you later after I go back to the resort and get everything set up."

He sighed, unsure what he should do. He didn't

want to miss the retreat, but he didn't want to leave Ava to deal with the police and the case alone—not when he was the only person who could partially identify the thief.

"Okay, you can stay," he said to Ava after he hung up.

She let out a sigh of relief. "I'll have to call Dawson when I get my phone back and personally thank him for being so nice. He had no obligation to give me special treatment."

Jeff plopped his duffel bag on top of Ava's suitcase and grabbed the handle. "Let's get a cab back to the resort and get our rooms back. In the meantime, you can call the phone company. There's an American Express office in the lobby of the resort so you can talk to them about your stolen card."

"I'm sorry, Jeff," Ava said apologetically. "You've missed your flight."

He stopped and gazed into her troubled eyes. "Don't worry about it. Your situation is more urgent than getting back to the states."

Chapter Five

Friday, September 4th

The Perfect Mess

AVA HAD ALL she could do to keep from crying all the way back to the hotel. What would she do without her purse and all of the important items she took for granted every day? She could use the phone in her room for now and get another credit card, but her driver's license was another matter. It felt strange not having her purse and out of sheer habit, she kept touching her shoulder where the strap normally hung.

Her head ached from the stress of such a bad day and she could only guess what her face looked like. As it was, she suspected her cheeks were probably beet red, an embarrassment in itself. Her tears had turned the mascara on her eyelashes into hard, little spears and it was flaking off every time she blinked. She couldn't wait to get back into her room and slip into a relaxing hot bath. Well, after she got another room, cancelled her credit card and called her mother.

If Jeff had noticed her state of disarray, he hadn't let on. He paid the cab driver once they arrived at the resort and got their bags from the trunk of the vehicle. Taking charge, he turned the bags over to a bellman and went straight to the registration desk to rebook their rooms.

Ava found the American Express office located in the lobby and reported her card stolen. The representative took her information and assured her she would receive a replacement within a couple of days.

After that, she sat in a comfortable wing chair in the lobby and called Lisa on Jeff's phone to tell her what happened as she waited for Jeff to handle the check-in paperwork. He returned a short time later and handed the bellman a tip after he informed the man of Ava's room number.

"Here you go," he said to her as he gave her the key card to her room. "They've already rented out all of the balcony rooms—like the one you had—so I insisted they give you a nicer one at the same price."

"Thank you." Ava smiled and accepted the room key in its little paper sleeve. "You didn't have to do that."

"It was the least I could do." He offered his hand, helping her up from the chair. "You've been through enough today."

They strolled to the elevator and when the doors opened, they walked in and waited for the bellman to push the luggage cart inside. Ava stood in the back of the elevator and watched the floor indicator blink as the car whisked upward.

The elevator came to a gentle stop on the fourth floor "Club Level," and the doors silently swept open, waiting obediently for the bellman to push his cart out into the hallway.

"Thank you again for all your help," Ava said to Jeff as she followed the cart out of the elevator. "I really appreciate it." The doors came together before he had a chance to answer, postponing further conversation until later.

At the end of the spacious hallway, the bellman held the door to Ava's new room. She entered and stared in awe at her fabulous accommodations—a junior suite. The large room had a king-sized, four-poster bed, a cherry wood armoire, a dresser and two small armchairs with a round table nestled between them. The painted walls were a soft gold with matching drapes and gold/beige patterned carpeting. She glanced toward the glass patio doors and discovered a covered balcony area. The doors were wide open, filling the room with natural light and revealing a wide balcony furnished with a bistro table and two wrought iron armchairs.

The bellman brought in her bags and set up her suitcase on a luggage rack. After pointing out the amenities in the room, including the mini-bar, the Bahamian man smiled. "Will that be all, Miz Godfrey?"

"Yes, thank you very much." Jeff had pre-paid him to bring up her bags.

As soon as the door closed behind him, she kicked off her shoes and fell backwards on the bed. Staring at the white ceiling, she drew in a deep breath, savoring the fragrance of exotic flowers in the lush tropical gardens below her balcony. In many ways, this island was truly a slice of heaven on earth. It was unfortunate however, she couldn't have spent her time here under better circumstances.

Stretching out on the wide, comfortable mattress, she closed her eyes for a moment. She needed to call her mother but had put it off until she'd had some time to think about how to describe the situation without sounding an alarm. Her mother was a chronic worrier.

The last thing Ava wanted to do was get Georgette, and consequently her dad, upset over a situation none of them could control.

She let go of her problems with a long sigh as her body began to relax. She'd nearly dozed off when the phone rang. Dragging her arm toward the nightstand, she grasped the phone and pulled it to her ear. "Hello?"

"Ava, is that you?" Her mother, Georgette, had a squeaky voice when she sounded anxious.

"Hi, Mom. Yes, it's me."

"Are you all right? I haven't heard from you in two days. Why haven't you been answering your phone?"

"I'm fine," Ava mumbled, racking her brain for a believable excuse. "My phone charger went kaput, that's all, so I can't charge it. I need to buy another one." She didn't know why, but after all these years she still experienced a pang of guilt whenever she lied to her mother.

"You don't sound fine. You sound stressed. Have you been crying?"

"No, Mom. I'm just tired." Ava sighed and threw her arm over her eyes. "I'm glad you called. Would you do me a favor?"

"Why? What's wrong?"

If I tell you the truth, you'll have a cow. That's what's wrong...

"Nothing is wrong. Would you mind sending my passport by Fed-Ex to the hotel?"

Georgette gasped. "Oh, my gosh, are you in trouble?"

Ava began to laugh out of sheer frustration. "No, Mom. I'm resting. Then I'm going to take a bath and have something to eat."

"Then why do you need your passport? Enchanted Island is a territory of the U.S."

Think! Quick! Why do I need my passport?

"I went swimming and forgot my license in my bathing suit pocket," she said, hoping it sounded plausible. "It got wet and came apart. Now it's ruined. So, I need my passport for an ID to get on the plane when I return home."

"Oh," Georgette answered, never questioning the fact that bathing suits rarely had pockets, if ever, or realizing that most people who went swimming stored their valuables in a watertight container on a nylon string around their necks. "Where do you keep it?"

"The passport is tucked inside my oversized Bible. You know—the one that's as big as a coffee table book. I put it there to keep it safe. The Bible is sitting on one of my nightstands."

"When are you coming home?"

Ava pinched the bridge of her nose with her fingers. She loved her mother dearly, but some days it became vitally apparent that she needed to get her own apartment. "When you send my passport, Mom."

"Oh, right. You're sure everything is fine?"

"Yes, everything is *wonderful*," Ava replied, trying not to lose her patience.

"How is Lisa? Did the baby come yet?"

"Not yet, but it will be soon. I'll send you some pictures when I get another ph—I mean, when I get my phone charged. Thank you for taking care of my passport. Call me when you send it off."

They talked for a couple minutes longer before Georgette decided to hang up and get busy hunting down that Bible.

Ava expelled a deep breath, glad she'd been able to get her mother to send her passport without telling Georgette the ugly truth about what happened to her driver's license. Things were bad enough without her mother worrying over the situation, too.

She wanted to spend the rest of the day soaking away her troubles in the tub with a glass of good wine, but she remembered how rude she'd been to Jeff the evening before and her conscience pressed upon her to make amends. He'd stepped in to help her at a time when she'd needed it the most and had even cancelled his own plans in order to assist her. Besides, she wanted to know more about him.

She picked up the phone and hit the button for the operator. The operator came on the line and connected her to Jeff's room. The phone rang several times, making her wonder if she'd already missed him. Perhaps he'd gone to the beach or to the bar for an afternoon drink.

On the fourth ring he suddenly answered, but he sounded a little rushed. "Hello?"

"I'm sorry to bother you, Jeff. I hope this isn't a bad time to call."

"Not at all. I was just leaving when I heard the phone ring." He laughed. "The door shut on me and it took me a minute to find my key. What's up? Did Sheriff Hall call you about your purse?"

"No," she said sadly, "not yet. I just wanted to ask you what your plans were for dinner. Last night I turned down your offer, but I'd like to take you up on it tonight— that is, if you still want to dine with me."

"Yes, I'd like that." His voice softened. "What time would you like to meet?"

She thought to check her phone and remembered she didn't have one any longer. "Um..."

"Is seven okay? Or is that too late for you?"

"Not at all," she said quietly. "That would be wonderful. Where shall we go?"

"It'll be my surprise. I'll meet you in the lobby at seven sharp."

A surprise? That sounded like fun. "Seven it is then. I won't be late. Bye."

Chapter Six

Friday, September 4th

The Perfect Evening

JEFF MET AVA in the lobby at exactly seven that evening. She walked out of the elevator looking radiant in a long taupe halter dress with a wraparound waistband that crisscrossed in the front, accentuating her small waist. She'd let down her long, thick hair, her curly tresses reaching nearly to her elbows.

"Good evening. You look lovely," he said as she approached him.

"Thank you," she replied, her eyes shining.

He gestured toward the side door. "Shall we go?"

She took his arm and accompanied him out of the lobby.

Perfect Match employees were advised when they were hired not to get romantically involved with any of their clients for a host of reasons, but mainly because Dawson strongly believed it created a conflict of interest. If a relationship ended badly, it had the potential to reflect negatively on the reputation of his company. As a manager, Jeff knew Dawson expected him to uphold a high standard of professional conduct as a leader for his team and his peers. He needed to keep things on a friendship level only with Ava, but that didn't mean they couldn't have a nice dinner together. He just wanted to lift her spirits.

He opened the door for her and, as she passed by, the crisp floral notes of her perfume wafted upward, filling the air with her scent. The folds of her long, shimmering dress gently flowed with the sway of her hips.

He swallowed hard and looked away.

It's only dinner for one night. She's a client...not a potential date.

They barely knew each other and it had to stay that way. His goal was to help her get safely back home. Nothing else.

They walked down a lighted path to the pier behind the resort and the Black Coral Restaurant. As the maitre d' led them through the open-air, over-the-sea restaurant, Jeff breathed in the freshness of the evening air and took in the unforgettable, panoramic view of crystal-clear turquoise water stretching toward a pink and blue sky along the horizon.

The tables, covered in white damask cloths with lit candles in glass hurricane holders, were each set for an intimate evening. Soft strains of Caribbean music filled the air, accompanied by the happy voices and laughter of the couples seated in this romantic outdoor dining room. The maitre d' suddenly stopped at a table and pulled out Ava's chair.

"Thank you," Ava said and sat down. She smiled as the maitre d' pushed in her chair.

"Enjoy your dinner, Madame. Enjoy your dinner, sir." The maitre d' dropped Ava's napkin on her lap and left.

Immediately, a waiter's assistant dressed in a black uniform appeared at the table. The young woman silently filled their water glasses and left as quickly as she'd appeared.

"How do you like your room?" Jeff said, attempting to keep the conversation light.

"It's wonderful." Ava sipped her chilled water

with a smile. "I love the balcony and the garden below is so beautiful. I have a small table out there and I think I'm going to have coffee delivered to my room tomorrow morning so I can sit in the fresh air and enjoy the sunrise."

A waiter appeared at their table wearing a black suit and tie. His nametag indicated he was Jamaican. He held a bottle of Chardonnay in his white-gloved hands. Smiling at Ava, he presented the bottle and said, "Good evening. I am Charles, your waiter. Would you like a glass of our featured wine tonight?"

Jeff gestured toward Ava. "It's your decision."

She looked up at Charles. "Oh, that would be lovely."

Charles opened the bottle and poured their glasses. After he left them, neither said anything for a few moments as they sipped their wine.

Ava relaxed in her chair, twirling the glass between her fingers. "How long have you worked for Perfect Match?"

Jeff set down his wine glass. "I've been with Dawson for about a year, since the company's inception. At the time, I had a job working strictly as a leisure travel specialist for a large travel agency. A friend told me about a new company he had applied for online and suggested I apply, too. I thought, 'What the heck, why not?' I had nothing to lose." He sobered. "I got a job with Perfect Match; my friend didn't."

"You must find great deals for yourself, but I'm sure everyone asks you about that. Do you travel a lot?"

Charles appeared at their table and handed them each an opened menu then proceeded to describe the specialty dish of the day, a seafood medley for two.

"I used to travel all the time," Jeff continued once Charles left. "I want to see the whole world. That's why I got into the business."

"But...you don't travel now?"

He lowered his menu. "Perfect Match is growing so fast, I'm too busy to take a vacation. I've just received a promotion and a new project so I'll probably have less time than ever now."

Ava's face lit up. "Really?" She looked radiant when she smiled. "Tell me about it."

"Dawson Yates is starting a regional office in Minneapolis and he's assigned me as the project manager. I'll also be the office manager when it's finished and our staff moves in."

Her lips parted slightly in surprise. "I didn't know you lived in Minneapolis. I live there, too." She blushed, obviously realizing she'd pointed out the obvious. "But then, you already know that."

He nodded and let it go.

Ava had begun to peruse the list of entrees when Jeff signaled for their waiter to return.

"Do you like seafood?" At her nod, he continued, "Do you mind if I order for us?"

"Not at all. Surprise me."

"We'll have tonight's specialty, the seafood dinner for two," he said to Charles and snapped his menu shut.

The conversation ensued until Charles brought an appetizer of tamarind-glazed fried calamari. Once they'd finished the first course, they shared a salad bowl of mixed greens with passion fruit-sweet ginger vinaigrette and a basket of fresh rolls.

As they ate, they talked about safe subjects such as fun times in college, where they had traveled, the books they'd read, the movies they'd seen...never once trespassing on sensitive, personal topics. Jeff wanted to know more about her, things that weren't listed on her profile, but knew it would be inappropriate to dig deeper.

Charles brought a platter containing seared scallops, Cruzan garlic shrimp, yellowfin tuna and a side dish of creamy asparagus risotto. They began to taste the food and had so much fun trying the entrees they ended up simply eating off the platter together instead of dividing it up and putting it on their plates.

"Oops," Ava said, laughing as she reached for a shrimp and the tines of her fork tinkled against his.

"Go ahead." With a grin, Jeff pulled his fork back. "You reached it first."

She speared the shrimp and popped it into her mouth. When she went to take another one, their forks clashed again, causing her to burst into a fit of laughter. "You can have this one."

Jeff picked up his wine glass. "I think I've had enough."

She picked up hers. "Me, too, but I'm having more fun than I've had in a long time!"

Laughing, they touched their glasses together and sipped more wine.

The sun's waning rays had completely disappeared, turning the sky to a deep blue as their waiter's assistant cleared away the dishes and Charles brought steaming mugs of coffee. He handed them each a small dessert menu and left them to pour over the luscious offerings.

Ava set her menu on the table and picked up her coffee mug. "I'm too full for dessert. How about you?"

"Frankly, I find most of the items on this list too rich and too sweet." Jeff set his menu down and pushed it aside. "I could use a bottle of water and a long walk instead."

"That makes two of us. We could go back to that garden we were at yesterday. It's next to the main building."

"Sounds good to me. Let's go."

They requested bottles of water from Charles' assistant and walked back to the main building, taking the sidewalk to the garden, now softly lit with LED lights placed along the curving walkway.

Ava had removed her high-heeled shoes and she walked barefoot most of the way.

"It's so beautiful here. I miss visiting exotic places. I used to travel a lot before I met my ex-husband," she announced suddenly. They passed a tall bush of magenta bougainvillea, a mass of sprawling branches growing along the walkway.

"Why is that? Was his job so demanding that it didn't allow time for travel?"

She responded with wry chuckle. "It was more like he didn't have time for me."

"I find that difficult to fathom." He stopped walking. "How could any man in his right mind not have time for you?"

Her sad smile glowed in the overhead light as she turned her face upward and looked into his eyes. "He's a vice president of a large corporation. Brian travels a lot for his job, so when he has time off, he merely wants to stay home...and work some more."

"Did you work alongside him in his corporation, if you don't mind my asking?"

"No," she replied sardonically. "I didn't work at all. Oh, I'd had a job before we were married. I worked as a flight attendant for Sunshine Airways. Actually, Brian and I met on a flight from MSP to O'Hare. We started dating and eventually he asked me to marry him. The problem was that he wanted me to quit working and stay home so we could be together more often. I didn't want to quit—I loved flying, but I thought I loved him more and so I did what he asked."

They began walking again. A light breeze picked up. He watched the warm wind scatter the curly wisps of hair framing her face, wondering how any man could treat her so selfishly.

"It didn't work out, of course, because it was doomed from the start," she continued. "You can't sustain a one-sided relationship. Brian was never home. I eventually became bored and unhappy with his work schedule. Then one day he simply dropped a bombshell revelation and blew up our marriage. He said I wasn't the woman he'd married. Over the course of two years, I'd become someone he didn't know any longer and he wanted a divorce." A rueful laugh escaped from her lips. "He'd demanded that I change and when I did, he didn't love me anymore. Many times, I've wondered if he ever did."

Jeff drained his water and tossed the empty bottle into a recycling receptacle next to one of the lights. "That must have been a tough situation for you. How did you handle it?"

"Not very well." She shrugged. "I had to start over completely. I'd left the only job I'd ever wanted and at the time, Sunshine Airlines wasn't hiring flight attendants, so I applied for a ticket agent position instead. I made it through all of the interviews and now I'm on a waiting list. In the meantime, I'm working for my father. My mother convinced me to move back home temporarily until I got my life back together and I hate to admit this, but it's been over a year and I'm still there."

"I understand you work with landscaping."

"Well, I don't actually do any of that," she replied. "I'm a manager at my father's garden center. He's the landscape architect. I handle the retail division."

"How is that working out for you?"

"Dad wants me to take over the business when he retires, but I'm certain I don't want to spend the rest of my life selling birdhouses and flats of petunias to suburban housewives."

"You like spontaneity. I could tell that the moment we met." He took her hands in his, gently pulling her close. "Your ex-husband was a self-centered fool. A woman like you would be an asset to any man."

She looked up at him with wide eyes, her lips parting slightly as though she didn't know how to respond to such a frank comment.

For a fleeting moment, he wondered how she would respond if he kissed her. His head dipped low, nearly brushing her lips before he realized his mistake. Reminding himself she was a client, he drew back. "It's getting late," he said. "Your feet must be tired. We'd better go inside."

She nodded and pulled away, but not before he'd caught a glimpse of disappointment in her eyes.

They walked back to the lobby in silence. At the elevators, Jeff pressed the call button and the doors opened.

"Thank you for meeting me for dinner," Ava said quietly as they stepped inside and he pressed their floor buttons. "I had a wonderful time."

"Will you be around for breakfast?" He spoke before he remembered that she had planned to call room service.

The doors closed and the elevator began to lift upward.

"Yes," she replied, surprising him. "It's actually my favorite meal of the day."

Don't ask her...

He ignored his inner voice and opened his mouth

anyway. "Would you like to meet me in the café, say around nine? After I've had my morning workout?"

"Yes, I'd like that."

The elevator stopped, the doors opened and Ava walked out. "See you then."

He held the door open for a few seconds, watching her hips sway as she walked away.

It's only breakfast...

Chapter Seven

Saturday, September 5th

The Perfect Ride

AVA RELAXED AT the bistro table on her balcony with a small pot of black coffee as she listened to the birds chirping in the morning sun. It seemed odd not to have a cell phone setting on the table next to her coffee mug, its constant *ping* reminding her to check her email, her Facebook account and the day's news, but at the same time, not having it gave her a sense of freedom. Never before had she realized how much she had come to depend upon that one tiny device—or how much of a slave she'd become to it. In a way, she wished she didn't have to get another one, but of course, that would be completely impractical. Her friends—and her mother— would have a fit if they couldn't call her, text her or message her.

As she sipped on her coffee, she gazed through

the bars of the iron railing to the lush tropical garden below. The same garden where she and Jeff had strolled the evening before...and he'd nearly kissed her.

Curious, she stood up and peered between the wide palmate leaves of the tall trees shading her room to gaze down at the beautiful foliage. An older couple held hands as they strolled along the paved walk curving between orange and yellow hibiscus shrubs and pink bougainvillea. In the distance, a small, white wedding chapel sat regally on a stone patio with tall white statues lining the walk leading up to it. Behind it, the sea stretched toward an endless horizon. She wondered if the couple had come here to get married or if they were celebrating a major milestone in their marriage. They looked so happy together.

She turned away from the railing, questioning why some couples were perfectly matched and others were not. Her marriage had fallen apart within two years, but the damage it caused had lasted much longer. She wished she'd known beforehand what she knew now about the necessity for give-and-take in a marriage, but unfortunately, she'd learned the hard way.

She was glad she had decided to accept Lisa's gift and make this trip. Some of it had turned out to be a total disaster—well, most of it, actually, so she couldn't understand why she had suddenly experienced such a burst of happiness in her heart. Could it be because she was looking down at a garden filled with the most beautiful magenta bougainvillea in a truly enchanted place? Was it because she had a good chance now to see Emma, Lisa's new baby?

Or could it be Jeff...

She shook her head. "Don't get any ideas, Lady. He's an employee from Perfect Match sent here to handle the mess you've made by kicking both of your matches off the island. Now that you're stranded, he's only staying with you out of a sense of duty to his company."

She sighed, knowing she'd hit on the truth. In a couple days she'd be back home and would never see him again.

The shrill ring of the telephone jarred her thoughts. She went into the bedroom, wondering if Jeff had changed his mind about their breakfast date. It wasn't Jeff calling, however. It was her mother.

"Hi, Mom, did you ship my passport this morning?"

"That's why I'm calling, honey. I can't find it."

What?

An instant hot flash swept over her, causing her to feel faint. She had no idea she could experience such a thing at thirty-one, but she'd never lost her only legal form of ID at such a crucial moment before, either.

"Did you check my large Bible? I *always* keep it there."

"That's the problem. I can't find it."

"Mom," she replied, beginning to panic, "it should be right on the nightstand where I left it. I don't see how you could miss it. The book is nearly as big as a carry-on suitcase."

Georgette sounded completely baffled. "Well, it's not there now."

"Did you look under the bed or behind the furniture?"

"Yes, I did. Are you *sure* you left it there?"

Ava sat on the bed and stared at the floor, racking her brain to remember the last time she'd seen it before she left for Enchanted Island.

Ohmygosh. Ohmygosh. Think. How could you misplace something that big?

"Mom, I desperately need my passport. You have to find it."

Georgette smacked her tongue against the roof of her mouth, indicating she was deep in thought. "Maybe I'll get your dad to help."

The notion of her parents snooping through every nook and cranny in her personal space was not a comforting thought, but in view of the current crisis, the sacrifice had to be made.

"Okay, but please call me when you find it. If I'm out of my room, leave a message and I'll call you back."

"Haven't you purchased a new charger for your cell phone yet?"

She closed her eyes in frustration. *I would if I had a credit card.* "No, I haven't had time. I have to go downtown Morganville to get one."

"When you do, be careful. There are always bad people roaming around, looking to take advantage of unsuspecting tourists. Goodbye now."

She almost choked. "Right. Bye, Mom."

Letting out a small, exasperated shriek, she fell back on the bed and closed her eyes.

This day had already fallen apart and she hadn't even had breakfast yet.

****

At nine sharp, Ava walked into the Starfish Café and found Jeff already sitting in a booth, drinking coffee and reading the newspaper.

"Good morning," she said, purposely sounding chipper. She didn't want her passport woes to ruin her day.

He smiled. "Good morning." His thick, curly hair looked damp, as though he'd freshly showered. He wore a gray T-shirt with "Pink Floyd" printed on it, jeans and tennis shoes. The snug fit of his shirt revealed a wide, muscular chest and solid biceps, making him look truly like a buff "surfer dude."

She had dressed casually today as well in a pair of light blue Capri pants and a white knit top with a round neckline. And tennis shoes. Her feet were still sore from wearing those gorgeous, but impractical four-inch stilettos last night and she'd decided to give her toes a break by putting on sensible footwear for one day. She'd woven her hair into a French braid.

A young server approached their booth and set a

tall glass of orange juice in front of Jeff.

"Good morning," the girl said to Ava and handed her a laminated breakfast menu. "Would you care for coffee today?"

"Yes, please."

The server left to fetch her beverage.

"What are you having," Ava mentioned absently as she studied the menu, looking for her favorite breakfast dish.

"Oatmeal, banana and raisins."

"What? You're kidding!" She looked up from her menu and laughed. "You strike me as a fried eggs and sausage guy."

"I eat more than my share of that stuff, but not today. I need some energy."

"Why?" His healthy menu choices intrigued her. "What do you have planned?"

He set the paper aside and picked up his coffee mug. "I've rented a motorcycle to take a drive on the coastal road today. If I'm going to stay a couple days, I might as check out the highlights. My clients are always asking questions about the amenities on this island. It's very popular."

Really? Disappointment overshadowed her upbeat mood. That meant she'd be spending the day alone.

"Oh."

He set down his coffee, studying her curiously. "Does that mean you'd like to come with me?"

"Maybe I do." She went very still, wondering if she had the nerve to get on his motorcycle. "Yeah..."

"You sound undecided. Have you ever been on a motorcycle before?"

"...no."

He sat back and perused her with a mischievous grin. "This should be interesting."

Ava drew in a tense breath. "You won't go fast, will you?"

"How about I just go the speed limit?"

"Don't you usually do that?"

His wicked grin told her all she needed to know.

The server appeared with Ava's coffee and took their breakfast order. She decided to get the same thing

Jeff ordered, hoping his power food would give her the mental stamina she needed to get on his motorcycle. She was afraid she might lose her nerve at the last minute.

"How's the passport issue coming along," Jeff asked while they were eating breakfast. He knew she'd talked to her mother about shipping it to her at the hotel. What he *didn't* know was that Georgette couldn't find it.

"It should arrive in a day or so." She slipped her hand under the table and crossed her fingers.

After breakfast, they walked outside to inspect the royal blue Honda, or "bike," as Jeff called it, that he had rented from a dealership in Morganville, the island's territorial capitol city.

He handed her a black, sparkly helmet and helped her put it on. During breakfast, he'd called the dealership and asked for a second helmet to be delivered with the bike.

After strapping on his own helmet, he rolled the bike off the trailer and looked back at Ava. "Are you ready?" At her nod, he turned the key and went through several steps then pressed the starter button. The bike roared to life. Jeff turned and patted the empty space behind him. "Come on! Get on!"

Her stomach flipped a one-eighty at the thought of riding on the back of that mechanical monster, even if she did have—in her mind—the best driver on the island taking her for a spin.

Shaking with fright, she cautiously lifted her leg over the bike and slid across the seat, twining her fingers for dear life around the belt loops on Jeff's jeans.

"Ready?" he shouted over the noise.

She nodded nervously, feeling as though her breakfast might come back up.

I'm so-o-o glad I didn't order eggs!

Jeff cranked the throttle and the bike took off. At the end of the resort entrance, he stopped, looked both ways and took a left turn on the blacktop, quickly increasing speed. After the first bump, Ava let go of her death grip on his waistband and wrapped her arms around his waist. She scrunched her eyes shut, preferring not to watch the world whiz by.

After a few minutes, she wondered where they were going and decided to peek, opening one eye. The beauty of the landscape left her pleasantly surprised. The forest had disappeared, giving way to a panoramic view of the sparkling aqua waves of the Caribbean Sea lapping upon a rocky shoreline. They continued along the curved coastal highway with the wind in their faces and the sun on their backs, covering long, flat stretches of road and sometimes, rolling hills. They drove past exclusive resorts, sprawling estates, an occasional hamlet, skirted the edge of Morganville and at one point, spotted a majestic yellow mansion with white gingerbread trim sitting high upon a hill.

They made a complete tour of the island then bypassed their resort, continuing for a while before Jeff signaled and turned left at a sign that read "LaBore National Park." He pulled into a parking lot and shut off the bike.

"I saw some information on this park back at the resort and decided it would be an interesting place to visit," he said as he slid off the bike. He removed his helmet and assisted Ava in taking off hers.

She slowly slid off the seat, trying to keep her balance, but her knees wobbled so much she nearly collapsed.

"Hold on to me," Jeff murmured as he slid his arms around her, supporting her. "You're not used to riding, but it'll get better."

The gentle strength of his arm embracing her,

pressing her against his chest created a flutter deep in her stomach. She held on as he curved his arm around her waist, guiding her across the parking lot. They took a walking path made of crushed shells to the interpretive center.

Once inside the air-conditioned, brick building, Jeff purchased a couple bottles of water and obtained a walking tour map of the park. They left the building and sat at a table in the outdoor café, planning their day.

"I think we should do some hiking," he said as he spread out the map. He pointed to a series of interconnecting trails and boardwalks that wound through a hardwood forest, a mango swamp, an area for bird watching and other points of interest. "Would you like to do that?"

Ava glanced up from the map and saw the encouraging look on his face. "Hey, you're looking at a girl who hiked both the Grand Canyon and Crater Lake in high school. I'm no sissy. Of course, I'll do it." Smiling, she stood up. "Let's go."

Jeff and Ava spent the morning hiking several miles, visiting points of interest and reading the informational way markers at designated spots. At lunchtime, they dined on chicken wrap sandwiches and sodas in the outdoor café.

They spent the afternoon taking a guided tour through the LaBore Museum, the huge, yellow mansion they'd passed on the way to the park entrance. The one-hundred-fifty-year-old house had been the plantation home of one of Enchanted Island's most prominent citizens, Anna LaBore, who had recently passed away at ninety-seven. Anna had bequeathed her home, her land and her fortune to the IPC, formally known as the Island Preservation Commission. Her Last Will and Testament had given specific instructions to the IPC to convert her family's estate into a museum and a park to preserve the natural beauty of the area and the wildlife habitat.

By the time they made it back to the resort, they were hungry for dinner, but also very tired.

Jeff parked the bike and locked up the helmets before escorting Ava into the lobby.

"I had a lot of fun today. Thank you for taking me along," she said as they walked into the elevator.

The doors closed behind them. Jeff pressed their floor buttons. "What are your plans for dinner?"

Dinner by room service and a nice, hot bath sounded like the perfect medicine for what ailed her. "I'm so tired and sore I can hardly walk. I think I'm going to soak in the tub and relax tonight. Maybe read a book. And you?"

The doors opened at her floor, but he reached out to hold them while they talked. "I'm thinking about ordering pizza and renting a movie."

She stepped out into the hallway, wishing she wasn't so beat she could barely talk. An after-dinner ice cream drink with him in the bar would have been a nice way to end her day. "Enjoy your movie."

"See you at breakfast? Same time?"

She smiled. "Okay. See you then."

She stood watching as the doors closed on him, wishing they'd met under different circumstances. They'd had a lot of fun today, mainly because they held the same interests. If Jeff had been a fellow client of the online dating company instead of an employee, perhaps their profiles might have made a perfect match.

Ava walked to her room, humming a tune, wondering what Jeff had planned for tomorrow.

Chapter Eight

Sunday, September 6th

The Perfect Mistake

JEFF MET AVA for breakfast the next morning in the Starfish Café at about the same time and in the same booth. He'd completed his workout, showered and arrived early, taking the liberty to request coffee and menus for both himself and Ava.

She arrived at nine o'clock sharp wearing a yellow and white print tee and solid yellow shorts.

"Morning, sunshine," he said and filled her mug with steaming coffee from the thermal pot on the table.

She'd twisted her thick, copper hair into a knot at the crown of her head, but wispy tendrils escaped around her hairline, framing her face. She looked ready for another day of exploring the island. At least, he hoped so.

"Good morning," she said with a beautiful smile

as she slipped opposite him in the booth. "What's on the agenda for today?"

"More exploring. Do you want to come?"

She blew on her coffee and took a cautious sip. "Sure, what do you have in mind?"

"I thought it would be fun to visit Turquoise Cove. I've been asking around about the best places to visit and all of the resort employees give it two thumbs-up."

"Okay!" She picked up her menu. "What are you having for breakfast today, more oatmeal?"

He pushed his menu aside. "Whatever you're having. This time you get to pick."

She shot him a playful grin. "Then I'd say you're having a Belgian waffle with strawberries and whipped cream."

H-m-m-m...

"Make mine banana with walnuts and you've got a deal."

She laughed. "Okay, you get the banana and I'll get the strawberries."

He loved the sound of her laughter and wondered how long it had been since she'd truly had lighthearted moments like they'd experienced in the last two days. She could have used the robbery as a reason to be depressed or angry, but in spite of it all, she'd managed to keep her sense of humor.

Dawson had been wrong about her. The woman he'd dealt with had been frustrated and unhappy. And yet, given the right environment, she wasn't like that at all.

After breakfast, they stopped by the America Express Office in the lobby and checked on the status of Ava's new credit card. The customer service rep cheerfully checked Ava's account and informed them the card was on its way.

After that, they climbed on the bike and drove along the coastal highway until they came to the turnoff for Turquoise Cove. The narrow dirt lane took them uphill through a dense forest to a huge clearing where a weathered limestone outcropping overlooked the water. At the west side of the parking area, they saw a small café perched in full view of the cliffs and, in the distance, a high, densely forested mountain with a zipline station erected at the top.

Jeff parked the bike and locked down their helmets. They were about to walk toward the restaurant when a scooter sped into the parking area. Jeff stopped. Something about that scooter looked familiar; it was the same faded green as the one he'd seen at the airport. He lifted his sunglasses and studied the driver. The man wore the same black bill cap and sunglasses as the thief had worn.

"Jeff," Ava said, sounding astonished, "isn't that the—"

"Yeah, I think it is."

He started to walk toward the man, but Ava clutched his arm and pulled him back.

"Don't approach him! Get out your phone and take a photo for the Sheriff."

Jeff pulled out his phone and opened up the camera, snapping a couple pictures, including one of the license plate. The driver saw him and turned around, speeding away. Jeff pulled out his wallet and searched for the business card of Sheriff Hall. After a quick call, they waited in the parking lot for the officer to arrive.

Fifteen minutes later, Sheriff Hall pulled into the parking area in his old jeep and got out of the vehicle, striding toward them.

"So, you got pictures of the da suspect?" His

sentences always ended on an up-note. "Good job. Let's have a look."

He viewed the images and made notes regarding their encounter. Jeff emailed the pictures to Sheriff Hall's official email account then slipped his phone back into the pocket of his cargo shorts and connected the Velcro under the flap.

The Sheriff received a call on his radio about an unrelated incident and tore out of the parking lot.

Jeff and Ava made their way to the restaurant for a soda. They sat by the window and watched people diving from the cliffs.

"Those people are crazy," Ava said as she sipped her cola. "How far down is it?"

Jeff shrugged. "It's not that bad. We should walk over there and take a look."

Ava gave him a skeptical frown. "There isn't anything to hang onto at the edge."

He chuckled. "No one seems to be falling off."

She shook her head at his lame joke. "No, they're jumping off like crazy people."

After they finished their beverages, they climbed

the well-worn pathway up to the cliffs. People were congregating in small groups, laughing and talking, many of them soaking wet. Others went straight to the edge and jumped off, whooping all the way down to the water.

Jeff took Ava's hand as they walked toward the edge. "It's beautiful down there, isn't it?" The water truly looked turquoise and as clear as a windowpane.

She moved closer to the edge of the cliff and gingerly stared down at the cove. "It must be at least a twenty-five-foot jump."

"Do you know how to swim?"

She snorted. "Ah, yeah. I was a lifeguard all through senior high and college."

"Really? Me, too." He tightened his fingers around her slender hand. "Do you like to swim in the ocean?"

"Oh, yes, I love it. I've already gone swimming several times at the resort."

"Great!" He grinned. "Then let's do it." He leaped off the cliff and pulled her with him.

At first, she gasped from sheer surprise then she screamed. "I'm going to *kill* you for this, Jeff Thomas!"

Down they went, feet first.

Splash!

They plunged into the cove, but quickly swam upward, breaking through the water at the same time.

As soon as she bobbed to the surface, Ava blew out a lungful of air and shook the water from her eyes. Without a word, she took off like a shot and swam toward the beach. Jeff quickly caught up to her and followed her out of the water. She ignored him and stomped away.

"Come on, Ava. Don't be mad—"

"Oh, I'm not mad," she said, whirling around, getting in his face. "I'm furious! How *dare* you pull me over the edge like that?" The last pin fell out of her hair and her thick mane tumbled down her back in Rapunzel-like fashion. "I'm soaking wet. Look at my shoes!"

He smiled sheepishly. "Hey, I am too, but you have to admit, that was quite a rush." The only thing that wasn't wet was his phone. It had an expensive waterproof case he'd purchased at the resort gift shop and he'd made sure it was tucked securely, along with his sunglasses, in the button-down pocket of his army green cargo shorts.

She swung her fist. "I'll give you a *rush*!" Turning away, she angrily marched toward the parking area.

"Look, I wouldn't have done it if you'd said you didn't know how to swim. I checked with you on that. Remember? I knew you'd be okay." He took her by the arm and gently turned her around. "I would never have left your side."

"You should have asked me first!"

"You're right. I'm sorry." He slid his arms around her in an effort to calm her, but her closeness sent a shock through his body so fast it stalled his thoughts, distracting him and he nearly forgot what he wanted to say next. "I promise I'll never..." He blinked. "...do it again."

"I'm soaking wet, my hair is a sticky, salty mess and—"

"You've never looked so beautiful to me."

"Jeff! You're not listening—"

He cut off her protest with a kiss. At first, he'd simply meant to distract her, but the moment their mouths came together, he knew he'd stepped over a line he should never have crossed. His heart began to slam in his chest. His arms, though securely curved around her slender waist, trembled with uncertainty. Did she truly want this or was he once again pushing her into something without her permission?

She hesitated and he took it as a clear signal to stop. He didn't know whether he'd upset her again or if his impulsive action had stunned her as much as it had affected him. Her answer came loud and clear as she slid her hands up his chest and began to press into him, her lips eagerly embracing his.

He pulled her close and kissed her deeply, knowing he shouldn't be going down this path, but his desire to take her in his arms overrode his common sense. He'd been tempted to kiss her ever since they stood in that romantic garden on his first night at the hotel. He wanted to know what it would be like to hold her close, to breathe in the scent of her, to taste the sweetness of her mouth.

Several people began to whistle as they passed by, distracting them and destroying the magic of the moment.

Ava pulled away and glanced around. "I think we should go."

He tried to take her hand as they began walking toward the parking lot but she shook it off and charged ahead of him. She reached the bike before he did and walked around to the other side, waiting for him to unlock their helmets so they could go on their way.

Her reaction proved he shouldn't have made such a public spectacle of his attraction to her. It was inappropriate and it only served to make their situation more awkward. Given the fact that she was already upset with him for making her jump off the cliff, kissing her in public just made it that much worse between them. Realizing his error sobered him, reinforcing the necessity to stick to business and stop playing around with Ava Godfrey.

They didn't speak again until they arrived at the hotel. Jeff roared into the parking lot and parked the bike. He got off first and offered her a hand, but she refused.

"I'm sorry about what happened at Turquoise Cove," he said softly as she slid off the bike. "All of it. You have my word, it won't happen again."

She removed her helmet and handed it to him then turned and walked into the hotel, never looking back.

Chapter Nine

Monday, September 7th

The Perfect Day

THE NEXT MORNING Ava walked into the Starfish Café at nine o'clock and quietly slid into the booth, facing Jeff.

He sat reading the paper and didn't react at first, as though mulling over how to react to her presence. Slowly, he lowered the paper just enough to reveal his eyes. His golden brows shot up at the sight of her sitting quietly with her hands folded.

She stared at what little she could see of him, trying to gauge his mood. "I'm sorry I got upset with you yesterday. I overreacted about jumping off the cliff at Turquoise Cove. I was never in any danger. I'm an excellent swimmer and that jump was a piece of cake, really."

But that kiss was amazing...

He didn't move. Instead he sat motionless and unblinking.

"I'm over it, okay?" She pursed her lips together, wondering why he didn't have anything to say. Had her refusal yesterday to accept his apology jeopardized their friendship? "No harm done. My shoes are dry...I even washed the salt out of my hair." She pulled at the elastic band holding her hair in a ponytail, letting her silky, thick mane fall past her shoulders. "See?"

He still didn't react.

"I mean, I've been on roller coasters that went up higher than that..." She held up her hands in frustration. "*What?!*"

"Are you saying you're ready to try it again?"

She countered with a wry chortle. "No, I'm saying I thought it was interesting and an exciting experience, but next time you get a crazy idea like that, ask me first, okay?"

He lowered the paper. "Do you want coffee?" At her nod, he signaled their server to come to their booth.

The server appeared immediately with an empty mug and a breakfast menu. She filled Ava's mug and left the thermal pot on the table.

Ava accepted the menu and perused the items as she sipped her steaming coffee. "What's on the agenda today?"

Jeff folded the paper and set it beside him on the seat. His blue eyes twinkled. "Well, since you don't want to go back to Turquoise Cove, I'm thinking we could do some snorkeling around a coral reef. How does that sound?"

"Yeah." Ava set down her menu. "That sounds safe, educational and exciting. What time do you want to leave?"

"Right after we eat our banana pancakes."

She laughed. "You mean, banana pancakes for you and strawberry crepes for me."

She finally got a grin out of him.

"Whatever makes you happy."

Later, while eating their breakfast, Ava suddenly remembered something very important. "Oh, by the way, my passport should be delivered today."

On Saturday night, she'd gone up to her room to find the message light blinking on her phone. Her mother had called to say that her father had found her Bible, sitting on a stack of books on the top shelf of her bookcase. Georgette had put it there a couple weeks ago while cleaning and forgotten about it. According to the message, her father had immediately taken the passport to the Fed Ex office and shipped it, just making the cutoff for guaranteed two-day delivery to the island by Monday. Ava had no idea if Fed Ex had overnight delivery to Enchanted Island, but it didn't matter anyway; her father was much too...thrifty...to spend that kind of money mailing a mere envelope on the super-speedy plan, especially since Perfect Match was footing the bill for her all-inclusive room.

"Great," Jeff said, but as he spoke, his expression went blank. He didn't need to stay now that her passport was on its way. Once her Am Ex card arrived, which she hoped would be today as well, she would have everything she needed to get home. She wondered if the same thought had just crossed his mind, too.

After breakfast, Ava went up to her room to put on her swimsuit and found the message light blinking again on her phone.

"Now, what?" She went to her phone, worried that something had happened to the shipment of her passport. Perhaps her father had made a mistake on the address. Highly unlikely with him, but Georgette could have given him a faulty address by mistake.

The message wasn't from home at all. It was from Lisa...

"Hey, Ava," Lisa said, sounding somewhat tired but happy. "I've had the baby! Emma Jo was born last night weighing seven pounds and one ounce. We're both doing fine. I was hoping you'd have another phone by now but your number is still disconnected."

Stunned, Ava sat on the edge of the bed, staring at the wall. She'd been so pre-occupied with her own situation she'd forgotten to call Lisa for the past two days.

That's what I get for paying more attention to a guy I'll never see again than my best friend.

"I'll be at the hospital for another day," Lisa continued, "so why don't you come and see us? If you'd rather wait until we get home, that's fine, but I don't know how much longer you're going to be on the island so I thought I'd give you a ring and update you on the news. Give me a call and let me know what your plans are. And let me know what the scoop is with your phone! Talk to you soon. Bye."

Her plans for the day had just changed.

She put on a pair of white leggings and a gold

blouse with three-quarter-length sleeves and a layered, chevron-style hem. She met Jeff in the lobby a little later than she'd planned on and found him waiting for her in the reception area, as they'd agreed. He frowned at her outfit.

"Is that what you're wearing to go snorkeling? It looks really nice on you, but it might be a little hot to wear on the beach."

She held up her clear beach bag. "I've got everything I need in here, but there's been a slight change of plans. I hope you don't mind. Lisa had her baby and I want to visit her in the hospital before we go to the beach. I'm so happy for her and I can't wait to see Emma!"

He did a double-take. "Is the baby okay? And Lisa?"

Ava laughed. "Of course, they are. Do you mind driving me to the hospital?"

"Not at all. If it's in Morganville, it's on the way to where we're going anyway. Let's go."

Jeff asked the concierge the name of the island's only hospital and brought up driving directions on his phone. They hit the coastal highway and headed for Morganville. They found St. George's Hospital on the west side. The small, two-story building had stucco walls in bright yellow with aqua trim. They went up to the maternity ward, a small area with only two double-occupancy rooms.

Lisa had the room to herself. She sat up in bed, eating a cup of fruit and watching television as Ava and Jeff walked in.

"Hi! I was just thinking about you," Lisa said with a squeal.

Ava exchanged hugs with Lisa and introduced her to Jeff, adding that he lived in Minnesota and worked for Perfect Match.

"I've been waiting for my American Express card to arrive. I hope it comes today so I'll be able to get another phone," Ava said. "I promise, you'll be the first person I call to try it out!"

Ava started to ask about the baby when a nurse entered the room carrying a small bundle and handed it to Lisa. Ava waited until the nurse left before she rushed to the bed to get her first look at Emma.

"She's beautiful," Ava said wistfully as Lisa pulled back the folds of the pink receiving blanket. Emma had a round face and an unusually thick crop of glistening dark hair.

"She just had a bath. Would you like to hold her?" Lisa held out the small pink bundle.

Ava took the baby in her arms and smiled down at the child's sleeping face, wondering what it would be like to have one of her own. Her heart yearned to find out.

A hospital volunteer came into the room to give Lisa a complimentary gift basket of baby items from the Island Women's Club. While Lisa spoke to the woman, Ava sat down next to Jeff with Emma in her arms and showed him the infant.

"I don't know much about babies, but she's a pretty little thing," Jeff said, smiling down at Emma. "She's got the same dark hair as her mother."

Ava looked up at him. "Do you have any children from a previous marriage or..."

He frowned at the question and shook his head. "No. I've never been married or in a serious relationship that resulted in producing a kid."

"Would you like to some day?"

He shrugged. "Maybe, if I found the right girl."

"I'll bet you'd make a great dad."

Their gazes met and held. After a moment, he cleared his throat and looked away, obviously feeling out of his depth in such matters.

Ava looked down at Emma once more and knew she'd never feel complete as a woman until she held a baby of her own. She didn't regret not having children with Brian because their marriage had gone south so fast and she never wanted her children to grow up in a broken home. Divorce often happened to the nicest people, and she couldn't be absolutely certain it wouldn't happen to her again, but the next time she decided to get married, she planned to make sure the man in her life was her true soul mate in every sense of the word.

Future intentions, however, didn't fix the present hole in her heart; a hole that only a baby of her own could fill. Her eyes suddenly misted with unintended tears. Nothing in the world could take the place of having her own child—not a better job or a big house or all the money she could spend. She'd always known that, but her desire had never seemed urgent until now. As she held Lisa's sweet-smelling little bundle close to her heart, she'd realized for the first time what she was truly missing.

"Hey," Jeff whispered as he slid his arm around

her shoulders. "What's with the long face?"

She hugged the baby tighter and looked down at the sleeping child.

"It'll happen someday. Before you know it, you'll have a couple of 'em running around." He pressed his temple against hers, and quietly held her close. His patience and understanding surprised her, giving her even more reason to think he'd be a great dad—and husband—to one lucky girl someday.

Embarrassed by her emotional reaction, she wiped the moisture from her eyes and swallowed hard. This was Lisa's happy moment and she didn't need to see Ava casting a gloomy pall over her joyful event.

Within a few minutes, more visitors arrived to see the new baby. Ava handed Emma back to Lisa and said goodbye but promised to visit them again before she left the island.

Jeff drove her to Turtle Cove, a popular beach for swimming and renting snorkeling equipment. The shallow nature of the cove made it ideal for all level of snorkelers to swim out to Bluebeard's Reef and enjoy the abundant variety of sea life.

Ava pushed back her thoughts about wanting a

baby as she changed into her swimming suit, stored her clothes in a rented locker and swam out to the reef with Jeff. She spent the afternoon observing the coral reef, teeming with sea life and the warm Caribbean water. She noted the different colors and sizes of tropical fish that populated the coral bed. Much to her delight, she also saw a couple stingrays, squid, barracuda and a half-dozen sea turtles grouped together.

The rental company had a flotilla of bright-colored rafts for rent. Ava and Jeff took a break in the afternoon, relaxing in the sun on a couple rafts. They took their time, floating lazily around the reef before slowly padding toward the shore.

For an early dinner, they got a beach-side table at one of the local restaurants along the cove, dining on Pina coladas and grilled shrimp.

The ride back to the hotel didn't take long and as they pulled into the parking lot, they saw the Fed Ex truck parked near the entrance with its flashing lights on.

As soon as they parked, Ava hopped off the bike and tore off her helmet. "I hope my American Express card and my passport are here!"

She handed her headgear to Jeff and hurried into the resort. At the American Express office, she received her card and breathed a sigh of relief. The woman managing the office had informed her yesterday that the package had been delivered to the island Fed Ex distribution center, but deliveries always ran a day behind. That, Ava knew, was because here people operated on *island time*. Simply put, on island time, people were laid back and life moved at a relaxed pace. Living on island time meant you weren't pressured by the clock and if you were a little late, so be it. Lisa had warned Ava that people here didn't operate at the same frenetic pace as they did on the mainland and not to be surprised if it took an extra day to get delivery of the card.

Despite the slight delay, she received the card with a sigh of relief. She had one issue taken care of with two to go. Now, she could get a new phone and cross another item off her list. That left one thing still unresolved, her passport. It should have been here today, along with her new credit card.

She asked the Fed Ex driver to check on it for her and found the package was at the distribution center. According to him, he could make a call to have the package held at the Fed Ex office and she could pick it up the following morning herself if she didn't want to wait for it to be delivered. She agreed and thanked the man.

She found Jeff in the lobby, patiently waiting for her. "Here it is!" She waved her card. "Now, all I have to do is show up at the Fed Ex office first thing tomorrow morning and I'll have my passport, too."

Hearing the words escape her lips gave her a moment of pause. She'd been waiting for days to get her life back in order so she could fly home, but at the same time, that meant her time with Jeff would end. In the couple days they'd spent together on the island, she'd had more fun than she'd had in years but knew it had never meant to last. He'd stayed on only because Perfect Match didn't want to leave her stranded on the island without money or identification. He had no obligation to continue their friendship once they arrived back home in Minneapolis.

"Would you like to meet me for another drink later at the bar? Maybe this time we could try a frozen daiquiri." She laughed. "I'm thinking strawberry for me and banana for you."

He frowned with disappointment as he shoved his hands in his pockets and walked alongside her to the elevators. "I'm sorry, but I can't. I've got a dozen phone messages I need to follow up on tonight and emails I have to address once I get back to my room. Dawson is starting to get antsy for me to wrap things up here and get back to the states."

"Okay," she said lightly, though her elated mood took an immediate nose dive. "I understand. Shall we meet again tomorrow for breakfast?"

He held the door, allowing her to entered the elevator first. "Sure. It'll probably be our last day on the island so we should order something special." He grinned. "Sausage and eggs."

Chapter Ten

Tuesday, September 8th

The Perfect Proposition

JEFF SLID INTO his favorite booth at the Starfish Café a few minutes early of his appointed time to meet Ava and ordered his usual pot of coffee for the two of them.

After talking with Dawson last night, he was grateful for one last day to explore the island and he wanted to make it his best one yet. He'd convinced Dawson to allow him to stay over for one more day at Dolphin Bay resort, citing the need to make sure Ava's passport was, in fact, waiting for her at the island Fed Ex distribution center.

Dawson agreed and pitched an idea of his own. Instead of flying back home to Minnesota, Dawson wanted Jeff to meet him in Miami on Wednesday to attend the grand opening of the newest branch of Perfect Match. Dawson considered it a valuable opportunity for him to observe the office layout, familiarize himself with all of the staff positions and spend a couple days in training under the tutelage of the Miami manager.

Jeff had immediately grabbed the last two seats for him and Ava on the Wednesday morning flight from Enchanted Island to Miami and also handled her connecting flight to Minneapolis.

He checked his company email while he waited for Ava to join him, saving the ones he'd need to reply to or work on later. One particular email from Dawson drew his undivided attention, however.

The company-wide email had been sent to all employees with "Return Receipt Requested," updating them on the company's policy with regard to clients. What Jeff read served as a warning to him to maintain the proper professional relationship with Ava, but it also left his heart greatly conflicted.

According to Dawson, another Specialist had ignored company rules and cultivated a relationship with one of his female clients. That relationship eventually went south for reasons only known to the female and two weeks ago, she'd filed a restraining order with her local law enforcement office, accusing the Specialist of invading her privacy by using her confidential profile information to harass her and stalk her. Whether it was true or not had no bearing on the fact that the Specialist violated his agreement with Perfect Match when he became romantically involved with her.

As a result, the Specialist no longer worked for the company and all employees were scheduled to be given sexual harassment/sensitivity training immediately, with a refresher course on a yearly basis.

Jeff knew he had to make a choice—Ava or his job. In the short time they'd known each other, he'd grown to care for her, but so far, he hadn't crossed any lines, except for the time he'd kissed her at Turquoise Cove. He'd realized his error and vowed he wouldn't do it again.

Ava slid into her side of the booth at exactly nine o'clock wearing a pair of aqua shorts and a white top with aqua trim. With her hair swept into a long ponytail, she looked ready for an exciting last day on the island. He wanted to spend it with her, but he knew that when she heard what he had planned, she'd be adamant about spending the day on her own. Under the circumstances, it was for the best, anyway.

She turned over her coffee mug. "So, what's on the itinerary for our last hurrah?"

He poured her coffee and set the thermal pot back

on the table. "Remember that forest-covered mountain we saw from the cliffs of Turquoise Cove? The one with the big platform built into it? It's called Devil's Mountain. I'm taking a drive out there today to ride the Diablo Zipline."

Her jaw dropped. "You're...what?"

"This is something I've always wanted to do." He leaned forward. "The Diablo Line is five hundred feet high. It comes down the mountain and goes straight across Jewel Bay, ending up on the other side."

She stared at him like he'd lost his mind. "Why do you want to do that?"

He grinned. "It's the ultimate thrill."

She looked practically shell-shocked at the thought of shooting across the bay clipped to a mere cable. "Oh." Swallowing hard, she silently picked up her menu and stared at it.

Jeff decided to let the matter rest and order his breakfast. He could see her disappointment in staying back at the hotel by herself, but he didn't know what else to say. This particular zipline had been on his bucket list for a long time. He *had* to try it before he left the island.

They didn't speak of the matter again until they

were eating their meal and he noticed Ava studying him curiously. "What's the matter?"

"Have you ever been on a zipline before?"

Her question caught him off guard. Earlier, she'd given him the impression that she didn't want to discuss it any further.

"Sure," he said after he'd swallowed a forkful of basted egg. "Quite a few times."

"Where?"

"Here and there, actually," he replied and selected a small packet of grape jelly from the caddy. He pulled off the seal and began to spread a thick layer on his toast. "I've been on cruise ships that had them—short ones, mind you—not like the ones I've been on in the states or in the Caribbean."

She swallowed a bite of her omelet. "Are they safe?"

He shrugged. "I'd say they're just as safe as white river rafting or skiing down a mountain slope." He paused before taking a bite of his toast. "The Diablo Line is an approved activity by several cruise lines and a long list of travel companies so it comes with good references. Why are you asking?"

"I don't know..." She looked conflicted as she stared at her plate and toyed with her hash brown potatoes. "I supposed you've done that, too."

"Done what?"

"White river rafting and skiing down a mountain slope."

"Yeah, I have." He drained his juice. "I'm a big fan of outdoor sports, but I guess you've already discovered that about me."

She looked down at her plate and finished her breakfast in silence.

After the server removed their empty dishes, Ava held her coffee cup with both hands and stared wistfully across the room through one of the large windows showcasing the crystal-clear waves of Dolphin Bay.

She sighed. "I used to be an adventurous person—before I got married. My husband had to travel so much for his job, he never wanted to go anywhere when he was home."

Her ex sounded like a first-class jerk, but Jeff kept his opinion to himself. He didn't need to remind her of what she already knew. "I'd say jumping off a twenty-five-foot cliff on the spur of the moment is quite adventurous."

"You know what?" Her face lit up with a smile. "I'd like to do that again, only this time I'll be ready for it and enjoy every moment of it."

Really?

"When I get back, I'll drive you out there—that is, if you're serious about it."

"Of course, I am." She hesitated. "But, um...what if I wanted to go with you to Devil's Mountain? Would you mind if I tagged along?"

A red flag went up in the back of his mind. He didn't think it wise to take her to a place where she'd be bored. "You wouldn't have much fun simply waiting for me. Depending on how busy it is today, by the time we get there, it could take hours to get through the process."

"Yeah..." Ava replied, staring at the ceiling as she chewed on her lip. "Well, maybe I want to try the zipline with you." She shifted her gaze to him. "Is it expensive?"

He froze. No way did he want to buy her a ticket only to have her back out when she realized she really didn't want to hang five hundred feet in the air.

"It's a hundred dollars for one turn." He leaned forward again. "Are you *sure* you want to do this?"

"Yes." She stared hard at him. "I *need* to do it. It's time I got off the sidelines and became a participant again." Gripping her mug, she drank the last of her coffee and set it on the table. "I can pay my own way now that I have another Am Ex card."

"The money doesn't matter," he said, taking her hand. "All I care about is that you have a good time."

"Then what are we waiting for?" She slid out of the booth. "I'll put my bathing suit on under my clothes and meet you in the lobby in fifteen minutes. Okay?"

"Okay." He stood up and shoved his hands in his pockets. "This should be interesting."

****

Before they could have any fun, however, they had to take care of business. They drove out to the island Fed Ex office in Morganville and picked up Ava's passport. Then Jeff drove her back to the resort so she could take it up to her room and store it in the small safe in her closet. He needed to make sure she had possession of her passport and had stored it in a secure place to ensure she had a proper ID to leave the island tomorrow. No way did he want her to take it with her to Devil's Mountain. Not with the island purse snatcher still on the loose.

Within the hour, they arrived at the foot of Devil's Mountain and parked the bike in a lot that had been carved out of the dense woods covering most of the mountainous area. They approached the ticket office, a small building situated at the end of a short path. Ava's hand shook as she paid her admission, but to Jeff's surprise and relief, she went through with it. Upon paying, they received their temporary bracelets to wear instead of an actual ticket and were assigned their appointed ride time.

From there, they approached another small building painted in Enchanted Island's official colors of bright yellow with royal blue trim and rented a small locker to store the items they didn't want to take with them on the ride.

Ava stored her bag with her personal items, but Jeff preferred to keep his phone and his keys tucked safely in the flap-covered, Velcro-secured pocket of his khaki cargo shorts.

They were directed to an area where employees "suited them up" in their double-clip, full-body harnesses along with their helmets. After that, they were directed to a holding area on the cove. Long benches facing the beach were positioned in the sand for the riders to wait for their next instructions. Jeff found two empty spaces for them to sit.

He slipped her palm in his. "Are you okay so far?"

She gave him a nervous smile but nodded as she squeezed his hand.

As they waited, they were given a safety briefing where they were informed to keep their helmets on and leave all "clipping and unclipping" of their harnesses to the expertise of their guides. After the briefing, they were shepherded to a cleared area among the trees where they encountered a zipline.

They followed their group up the stairs to a metal platform where they waited in line for an attendant to get them set up.

"Are you ready?" Jeff asked Ava as they stood side-by-side, clipped in and ready to take the ride.

She took a deep breath and clutched the side bars of her attachment clipped to the cable trolley overhead. "Yeah."

And they were off.

Ava screamed at first, grabbing Jeff's attention, but her fear turned quickly to uncontrollable laughing as she soared down the hill, feet first with her hands gripping the sidebars connected to her harness for dear life. The ride only lasted about twelve to fifteen seconds, barely enough time for him to get settled once he took his attention off Ava. They reached the wide, wood landing as their trolleys slid into the landing zone, coming to an abrupt stop.

Dangling from her harness, Ava threw her head back and laughed again, obviously enthralled with her new adventure.

The visible change in her made him do a double take. Three days ago, he wouldn't have entertained the possibility of taking a swim with her much less a zipline ride on Devil's Mountain. When he first met her, she was an unhappy, uptight client who'd caused Dawson more problems than he could count. Jeff could have concluded his business with her and walked away without a second thought. But today...

The guide unhooked Jeff first, giving him a chance to get his bearings so that when Ava put her feet on the ground, he could assist her in regaining her balance. She leaned against him as they walked arm-in-arm off the platform, steadying each other.

She looked up at him, her eyes sparkling, her smile wide with exuberance. "That was great! And it wasn't scary at all!"

"Ava, that was just a warmup run." He gazed down at her. "The real thing is still to come."

Chapter Eleven

The Perfect Thrill

AVA FOLLOWED JEFF to the open-air bus that transported them up the mountain to the Diablo Line. The bumpy ride took them out of the public zone, through a fenced-in area secured by a massive set of solid metal gates attended by several guards. Though it was probably a necessity to keep the ride secure from vandals and the curiosity of the public, it created an atmosphere of secrecy, like she'd seen in the movie, Jurassic Park.

Once they arrived at the top of the mountain, they exited the bus and traveled a long, metal bridge with high railings between the tops of the trees to the platform, five hundred feet above sea level. The manmade rig reminded Ava of a giant erector set that her cousin Harry used to play with when they were kids.

Her tennis shoes tapped on the metal as she walked toward the platform, but she avoided looking down. Seeing how high up she was would surely make her nerves jangle more than they already did and she didn't want to frighten herself into changing her mind.

At the end of the walk she encountered two guides standing in a covered area, a man on the left side and a female on the right. The female guide waited for them at the top of a small stairway. Above her head a large sign read "PLEASE STAY BEHIND THE RED LINE – KEEP CENTER CLEAR." They turned to wait in a covered holding area behind the red line, but at that moment, the guide waved them on to the platform.

"Hi, are you team number one? Come up here, please," she said with a Bahamian accent as she stood aside and allowed Ava and Jeff to climb the short stairs to where she stood. She grabbed the "tail" on the back of each of their harnesses and clipped them to a "wire rope" safety cable running along the narrow-edged platform. "Follow me, please."

The male guide turned toward the small group of people waiting in the holding area and gestured toward the other side of the platform. "All right, number two team can come up..."

Ava's heart began to slam in her chest as she walked along the narrow platform. Her knees were ready to buckle.

They followed their guide to the spot where they were to be hooked to the actual Diablo Zipline. Ava stood next to Jeff, facing the bay, but rather than allowing her fear to consume her, she held on to her safety line and concentrated on the breathtaking, once-in-a-lifetime view. From up here, she could see the vast Caribbean Sea stretching for miles and miles. In the distance, the aqua water gradually turned to light blue where the sea met the sky at the horizon. To her left, on the other side of the sandy point, a large cruise ship majestically hovered in the water. Looming in the background behind it, forest-covered mountains jutted out to sea, their tops shrouded in misty clouds.

The guide hooked Jeff's harness to the trolley on the cable that would take him down the line. She walked over to Ava and connected Ava's harness to her trolley. Ava shifted around in it, trying to find a comfortable spot when the harness began to swing back and forth slightly. She went still, holding onto the side bars.

This is it...no backing out now. Breathe...

They waited for team two to be hooked up to their trolleys.

"All right guys, get in your landing positions,"

their guide instructed. "That's good," she said as she checked on Ava and Jeff. "Excellent."

Ava glanced over at Jeff. He sat quietly in his harness, looking calm and relaxed, but he didn't turn and look her way.

"Landing zone, landing zone," the guide called, speaking on her radio to someone on the other end of the zipline. "...this is the flight deck." Someone at the landing zone told her to "stand by."

They waited for a few seconds then suddenly, the order came from the landing zone to release the next set.

"Copy that...sending four!" The guide turned to Ava and Jeff. "Are you ready, guys? Let's go!"

Before Ava had time to grasp what was happening, off they went, both teams of two, speeding down the zipline, hurtling faster than a ride on a roller coaster.

The pressure of the fast, downward thrust made Ava want to scream but the view beneath her held such incredible beauty that at first, she could only gasp for breath as she stared in awe. Soaring down the mountain with the wind in her face, she sat still, her hands clinging to the side bars, her gaze taking in the umbrella-shaped treetops of verdant, tropical forest below.

Ohmygosh... Ohmygosh...

The experience mirrored a simulated hang glider ride she'd once taken at Disneyworld, coincidentally called *Soaring*, but this was so much more because it was *real*.

The forest flew by under her and Ava soon found herself gliding high over the beach, observing the canvas cabanas and the swimmers below, all the while descending lower and lower. She passed across the azure waters of the bay, the wind still rushing at her face as giant white caps roared beneath her, unfurling toward the shore.

The line gradually descended to only a few feet above the water, bringing her closer to the other side of the bay. With the landing zone in sight, she began to whoop loudly with joy, letting Jeff know how much she'd enjoyed the ride. He'd arrived ahead of her and still hung from his harness, waiting to be unclipped from the line.

Her trolley began to automatically decelerate. She glided toward the covered landing zone and saw the huge words painted on the front, reminding her to keep her knees up and apart as she slid in and made contact with the breaking mechanism. Laughing with hysterical happiness, she swung back and forth from the impact, waiting to be unclipped.

Once Jeff had been unclipped from his trolley, he stood nearby, waiting for her. When she finally landed on her feet, her knees nearly buckled.

"Whoa! Careful now." He reached out and caught her, sliding his strong arms around her waist. "Hold on to me."

Ava threw her head back and laughed again. She would have danced around if she'd had the energy. "I did it," she cried breathlessly. "I really did it!"

"I told you it was the ultimate thrill," he said, grinning like a little kid.

"It's the most exciting thing I've ever done, but it won't be the last." Ava slid her palms up his chest, loving the secure feeling of being in his arms. "I've been missing out on so much for a long time, but I'm never going to let go of my love of adventure *ever* again."

His eyes shone, gazing deeply into hers as he whirled her around, lifting her feet off the ground. She tightened her grip around his neck and pulled closer to him, showing him that this time she *wanted* him to kiss her, but as soon as she moved close, he stopped and set her down. Removing his arm, he took her hand instead and began to walk toward the bus to take them back to the parking lot.

His gentle rebuff confused her.

What's wrong with him? He didn't act this way at Turquoise Cove. What's changed?

Their attraction to each other had grown with each passing day. The kiss at Turquoise Cove—she knew he'd meant it, but at the time she was so shocked and upset about the surprise jump that she'd let it go. Had her angry reaction put him off? If so, her move a moment ago should have given him the proof he needed to know she had forgiven him.

But...had he forgiven her for the way she'd treated him in return? She wished she knew the answer.

Chapter Twelve

Tuesday Evening, September 8th

The Perfect Disaster

THEY LEFT DIABLO Mountain and drove straight to Turquoise Cove. Ava surprised Jeff by jumping off the cliff and into the water not once, but three times. Even more surprising, she seemed to enjoy it more each time.

They were walking toward the parking lot to drive back to the hotel when he received a phone call from Sheriff Hall.

"We're on our way," Jeff said and hung up.

"The photos we gave the sheriff provided him the lead he needed to find the thief and make an arrest. I guess they've recovered a lot of stolen property," Jeff said as he unlocked their helmets and handed Ava's to her. "I guess the guy had a small mountain of bags in the middle of his living room that he'd ripped off unsuspecting tourists."

Ava pulled her wet hair back and wound an elastic ponytail holder around it. "Really?" She put on her helmet and slid across the back of the bike. "Let's go!"

Twenty minutes later, they pulled up to the police station, a square building with open windows.

What, no air-conditioning in this building?

They walked into a medium-sized room, divided into cubicles. Oscillating fans were strategically positioned to keep the air moving. Overhead, the rattan blades of a ceiling fan spun around, making a slight clicking sound. Even with all the moving air it was still hot in there, but the people on duty didn't seem to notice.

Jeff approached a woman sitting at the front desk answering the phones. "Hello, we're here to see Sheriff Hall."

The sheriff suddenly appeared from his cubicle. "Good day. Please, come with me."

They followed him back to his office and sat down, waiting there as he disappeared into the Property Room to look for Ava's purse.

They were fanning themselves with a couple brochures when Jeff's phone beeped, alerting him he had a text waiting. It turned out to be Dawson, but just as he started to read it, the door opened and the sheriff returned with a peach-colored Kate Spade brand bag. An identification tag hung on a string tied to the handle.

"Is this yours?" He held it out. "It fits da description you gave me."

Ava checked the bag's official ID number. "Yes, thank you!" She smiled happily and accepted the purse. She promptly opened it and looked inside. "It's empty," she said with disappointment.

"I am sorr-ee, Miz Godfrey. That is all we recovered. Da thief had a lot of handbags and beach bags, but most of them were emp-tee."

Ava signed the appropriate paperwork and thanked him for recovering her purse.

"At least you got your purse back," Jeff said as they walked out of the building. He breathed a sigh of relief, ironically, to get outdoors and into cooler air.

She slung it over her shoulder. "It's my favorite so I'm glad the police recovered it."

"You need something to put in it, right?" Jeff walked up to the bike and unlocked the helmets. "Let's go get you a new phone."

She looked surprised. "Are you sure? I don't even know where you'd get a new phone around here."

He held out her helmet. "There's a store in downtown Morganville. I looked it up and, yeah, I'm always game when it comes to shopping for electronics."

He drove Ava to the island's single phone store and helped her find a new one at a fair price. At the same time, he looked around, shopping for a possible new model for himself.

The crimson sun dipped below the horizon, shooting streaks of gold and orange light across the early evening sky by the time they returned to the resort.

"Breakfast tomorrow?" Jeff asked as they walked toward the entrance. "We'll have time if we get there early."

"Sure," Ava replied. "I'm going to get packed as soon as I get back to my room."

Jeff's phone beeped again. Another text from Dawson. With all the shopping going on, he'd forgotten to read the first one. Concerned, he quickly swiped the screen. The first text informed him of a change of plans. The second one was merely Dawson requesting confirmation.

Jeff stopped in the center of the parking lot, staring at the words.

Ava continued on, but stopped at the entrance and turned around, frowning at him. "What's wrong?"

"I just got some news from Dawson."

"Oh?" She walked toward him. "You look surprised. What sort of news?"

The moment I always knew was coming, but I didn't expect it to come tonight...

He truly didn't want their time together to come to an end, but he didn't show it. "There's been a change of plans," he said, keeping his voice even. He shoved his phone back into his pocket. "Dawson wants me to catch the ferry tomorrow instead of flying. It gets into Miami earlier in the morning and I need to meet him as soon as possible because we've got a full schedule for the day and the rest of this week."

Even though it was a short hop from the island to the mainland, flying and getting through two airports would waste most of the day and Dawson wanted him to arrive at the Miami office's open house as early as possible. Jeff had hoped he could have enjoyed breakfast with Ava one more time, but the ferry left the island at eight in the morning. The restaurant didn't open until seven, the same time he'd be at the dock, buying his ticket.

She stared up at him, a lonely, faraway look present in the depth of her eyes. "Then I guess this is goodbye."

Chapter Thirteen

Tuesday Evening, September 8th

The Perfect Move

AVA'S GAZE LOCKED with Jeff's, desperate to understand him. He'd been backing off emotionally all day and she didn't know why.

The past two weeks on Enchanted Island had been the most turbulent—and the most wonderful time she'd had in years. What started out to be the "perfect mismatch" had turned into an adventure she'd never forget. She'd come to the island with an attitude of skepticism and fear, but the events of this week had changed her. Being with *him* had changed her.

But now, judging by the blank stare in his eyes, this was *truly* goodbye. It disappointed, frustrated and angered her. He was polite, but his demeanor had reverted back to the first time they met and he'd introduced himself as a representative of Perfect Match.

In other words, their relationship had been reset to a professional one only.

So be it. Life goes on. I'm not going to let him break my heart.

She held out her palm to shake his hand, determined not to let her true feelings show. "Thank you for all you and Perfect Match have done to help me recover what I lost. I appreciate your assistance." She pasted a smile on her face. "Have a good trip."

Before her feelings could betray her, she turned and walked into the resort, resolved not to look back. She hurried through the lobby looking straight ahead, concentrating on not showing her feelings in public. The moment she entered the elevator and the doors closed, however, her bravado fell apart. Alone at last, she burst into tears.

"This is stupid. Why do I care?" She argued aloud as she folded her arms and leaned against the wall. "I'm getting all emotional over a guy I've only known for a few days. Sure, we had some good times, but I guess that doesn't mean he'd want to see me again once we both got back home." Stifling a sob, she tossed her hands in the air. "So, it didn't work out. The experience did serve to make me realize something, though. I've got to get on with my life—starting now."

As soon as the words tumbled out, she felt as though a huge burden had been lifted off her shoulders. For the past year she'd been living at her parents' home, working for her dad and basically hiding from the world. Her divorce had not only destroyed her morale, but her faith in true love as well. Getting away from her issues had allowed her to see what she'd been too angry and depressed to realize all along—changing her life began with changing her *attitude*.

The doors of the elevator opened and Ava walked out into the hallway, feeling like a different person. She strode purposefully to her room and went inside then kicked off her shoes. She poured herself a glass of Cabernet and walked out to her balcony to relax at the bistro table and enjoy the nighttime view of the garden for the last time.

Tomorrow, she planned to check out early so she had time to visit Lisa and the baby on her way to the airport. At the terminal, she'd buy a notebook and start planning her future. A new job, a new place to live...

Her phone beeped.

Out of habit, she pulled it from her pocket and swiped the screen. It was the first time she'd looked at the phone since the sales rep at the store set it up for her. She didn't want to tackle the hundreds of emails waiting for attention, plus texts and voicemails. She set the phone on the table and shoved it away.

Not now...maybe later.

Another situation she planned to change. No more living from email to email or text to text.

Her hand must have accidentally connected with the voicemail icon because a voice suddenly asked for her pin number. Wondering if the pin actually worked, she tapped it out and hit enter. Voicemails began to flow on her new speakerphone. She moved to end the session, but her hand stopped mid-air as she froze, listening intently. An HR Specialist from Sunshine Airlines had called to offer her a job as a ticket agent and left the information to call back. If she accepted, her training would start in a week.

She let out a whoop of joy. Halleluiah! She couldn't wait.

****

Tuesday Morning, December 2nd

Minneapolis, Minnesota

Ava stood in the living room of her new

apartment and stared at the boxes strewn across the floor. She had two days to get her place in order before she had to go back to work.

She'd been at her new job at Sunshine Airlines for three months now and loved working at the airport again. Once she'd finished her training and started her regular shift, she began earnestly looking for a place of her own. She loved her parents, but she needed her own space. They'd helped her move everything from her bedroom and the garage. Now it all sat piled up in her living room.

She stared out her picture window to the freshly fallen snow covering the city in a pristine blanket of white powder. It seemed like ages since she'd visited Enchanted Island and she wondered wistfully what Lisa was doing this very minute. Probably sitting on a beach somewhere under an umbrella with Emma.

I miss her so much. And the island. I'll never forget the exquisite beauty of that place.

Such thoughts made her uncomfortable. Every time she envisioned any aspect of Enchanted Island, she was reminded of Jeff. She hadn't spoken to him since the last time she saw him and that's where she wanted to leave it.

Pushing him out of her mind, she picked up a box

and began to unpack.

By early that evening, she had her living room cleaned, pictures hung and most of the boxes emptied. In one corner, she'd set a small Christmas tree on a square table. The three-foot tree had white flocking and multi-colored lights, the perfect size for her apartment. She plugged it in and turned off the living room lamps.

Home sweet home, apartment style.

She poured herself a glass of wine to celebrate and relaxed on her sofa, enjoying the coziness of her new home.

Her phone rang. Annoyed at having her peace interrupted, she glared at the screen. Oh, it was Lisa.

"Hey, you," Ava said cheerily. "Merry Christmas!"

"Merry Christmas to you, too, and congratulations on your new apartment," Lisa said. "I suppose you're busy unpacking. I won't keep you long."

Ava laughed. "I'm finished for the day. I'm sitting on the sofa with a glass of wine and trying to figure out how to work the remote on my new TV." Setting down her wine glass, she picked up the remote, examining the buttons. "When are we going to get together again?"

"That's what I'm calling about. Shawn and I are

flying to Minneapolis next week with the baby and getting a room at the Radisson Blu at the Mall of America. We thought it would make a nice family getaway for Christmas to visit a place with real snow and at the same time, we'd get some shopping done. Want to spend a day with us?"

"Of course, I do! Name the day and I'll be there."

In the background, Emma began to fuss. "How about next Wednesday?"

"Sounds perfect. I get Wednesdays and Thursdays off. What time?"

"Let's meet after breakfast. We can catch up on each other while Emma takes her morning nap." As if on cue, Emma began to wail.

"Okay, see you then!"

Good, Ava thought happily after she hung up. *We'll have a nice relaxing day together.*

****

Wednesday, December 10th

Mall of America, Bloomington, Minnesota

Despite being a weekday morning, the noise in the Mall of America rose to a deafening roar. People shuffled along elbow to elbow, no matter what floor Ava and Lisa traveled in the massive, four-level shopping complex. The mall housed over five-hundred shops, sixty restaurants, a movie theater, several hotels and an amusement park that took up the entire center courtyard. Oddly enough, the noise didn't seem to bother Emma. She smiled sweetly for her picture with Santa. After that, Lisa gave her a bottle and put her down for a nap. Lying peacefully under a fuzzy blanket in her bassinette stroller, she slept through it all.

They'd been shopping for several hours when Lisa suggested they take a break and get some ice cream. But not just any ice cream. She wanted to stop at "Hannah's Homemade Ice Cream Shop." She'd purchased a fudge brownie ice cream sandwich at Hannah's the previous night and desperately craved another one.

"Oh, my gosh," Lisa exclaimed as she maneuvered Emma's stroller through the crowd. "They take a pair of warm, homemade brownies and put a thick slice of frozen vanilla ice cream between them. It's soooo good. You can even get a side of hot fudge for dipping."

It sounded like major sugar overload to Ava as she gestured at the enormity of the mall. "How in the world could you find an ice cream shop in this place?"

Lisa pointed straight ahead. "It's on this floor, right around the corner."

They were on the ground floor and had just passed a large bookstore. Ava made a mental note to go back there after they loaded up on ice cream and coffee. If she didn't, she knew she'd never find that place again.

To her dismay, the extensive line at Hannah's suggested they were in for a long wait, but that didn't seem to deter Lisa. She pulled Emma's stroller toward the store and took her place behind the last person. Ava reluctantly fell in behind her. She slung her handbag over her shoulder and sighed, wondering how long they'd be stuck here.

"Hi!"

The voice sounded familiar, but Ava couldn't quite place it.

"Come on in!"

She looked to her left and saw Amy Sheridan, Lisa's friend from her Romantic Hearts Book Club, smiling and waving from inside the entity next door. The place had an exquisitely furnished reception area with oriental rugs, beautiful artwork and beige sofas facing each other in front of a huge electric fireplace. Toward the back were individual offices walled in with glass.

What is this place? What's Amy Sheridan doing there?

Amy was engaged to Dawson Yates, owner of Perfect Match. Behind Amy, Dawson Yates and Lisa's husband, Shawn Wells, stood chatting next to a long buffet table.

Ava took a step back and looked up. The sign above the wide entrance read "PERFECT MATCH Online Dating and Travel Agency." She blinked... *W-what?* This was Jeff's office—the one Dawson Yates had promoted him to set up and manage.

Realizing Lisa had brought her here on purpose, she quickly grew uncomfortable. She had a mind to turn around and walk—no—*run* away, but Amy had already hurried out to meet them.

Amy looked beautiful in a black velvet dress and matching shoes. Her dark, curly hair had been swept into a pretty chignon at the nape of her neck. Her green eyes sparkled. She approached Ava and took her by the arm. "Today is the grand opening of the Midwest branch of Perfect Match. Come in and see our newest agency."

Ava stared at Lisa, hoping she'd object as Amy

pulled her out of line and into the office. Instead, Lisa left her place in line, too, and followed them. Amy gave them both a little history of the company along with a brief tour, but Ava barely heard her. Once she saw Jeff, her heart began to race.

He stood off to one side talking to someone, perhaps a prospective client. He looked so different in his dark suit and short haircut, but no less handsome than when he wore shorts and a T-shirt. Seeing him brought back a rush of memories and at first, she couldn't take her gaze off him. The happy times they'd shared on Enchanted Island—and sadly, left there—pierced her heart.

Amy pointed to the buffet and invited the girls to sample the hot and cold appetizers. She handed Ava a glass of red wine. "Enjoy the party!"

Ava thanked her and turned away, hoping no one would notice how badly her hands shook. She desperately hoped Jeff wouldn't see her though the crowd of people milling about the agency. She planned to stay out of his line of sight until she could convince Lisa to leave. That fudge brownie ice cream sandwich with a hot fudge dip was sounding better all the time.

Unfortunately, Lisa didn't seem to have much

interest in getting back in that line for ice cream any time soon. She'd joined her husband, Shawn and was conversing with one of the matchmaking specialists on the Minneapolis staff.

I can't stay here. I know what Lisa and Amy are trying to do and it won't work. It's embarrassing, to say the least. I need to leave before he sees me and thinks I'm in on their ill-conceived plot to force us together.

"It's too crowded in here," she said to Lisa. "I've got to get some air."

"Where are you going?" Frowning with disappointment, Lisa handed Emma to Shawn. "Why don't you want to stay and enjoy the party?"

"I'm going to the Disney Store. We passed it on the way here and I saw an outfit I want to get for Emma." She avoided Lisa's second question. Both of them already knew the answer. She handed Lisa her untouched wine. "Call me when you're ready to meet for dinner."

"What about the baby," Lisa called after her. "I thought you wanted to hold her for a while..."

Ava hated to ignore her best friend, but she was desperate to leave. She wove her way through the heavy crowd to the opening to the mall. Out in the mall, the conditions were worse. Thousands of people roamed the wide corridors, talking and laughing, many shuffling along like holiday shopping zombies. The sheer number of stores in this mall proved enough to put anyone in merchandise overload. Loudspeaker music, ecstatic screams and the heavy rumble of amusement rides in the mall's four-story, center courtyard echoed throughout the entire complex.

She slowed down once she entered the corridor and breathed a sigh of relief as she strolled along, gazing at the newest fashions in the women's dress shop next door.

"Ava, wait!"

She froze. Even in the midst of this craziness, there was no mistaking that voice.

Slowly, she turned around and gazed into his sober face as he approached her. His eyes were bluer than she remembered. They searched hers with a profound loneliness that penetrated deep into her soul.

Her heart skipped a beat. All the hurt and disappointment she thought she'd dealt with back in Enchanted Island came rushing back, stronger than ever.

Chapter Fourteen

Wednesday, December 10th – Mall of America

The Perfect Fool

HE COULDN'T BELIEVE she was leaving already.

She looked as beautiful as ever in black skinny jeans and a silver, metallic top. Her thick, coppery hair cascaded over her shoulders and glistened in the light. Just standing near her made his heart slam with anxiety, but he could see by the fire in her eyes she didn't feel the same. She looked downright upset and he didn't blame her. After the way he'd left her on Enchanted Island, she had every right to despise him.

But he wanted to make it right. Now that he had the chance, he wanted her to know why he'd backed off and left her there without further commitment. He owed her that much. He owed it to himself to tell her the truth—about everything.

"How have you been?" he managed to say, though he couldn't hold back a slight hitch in his voice. "You look amazing."

"I'm fine," she replied curtly.

"Thank you for coming to the open house. It's nice to see you again."

She didn't answer, letting him know he sounded like a rambling idiot.

"Ava, I—"

"Don't..." Her hand shot up to silence him. "I said, I'm fine. Leave it there."

Sweat began to form on his upper lip. He hadn't anticipated she would so swiftly and blatantly reject him.

"I've missed you." He moved close. "Please, don't shut me out. May I walk with you?"

"What about the open house? You should get back to your clients."

"I need a break." He looked into her angry, hazel eyes. "Besides, I want to talk to you."

"Seems to me, we said everything we needed to say the last time we were together."

She began to walk away, but he fell in beside her,

determined to get through to her. "I'm sorry," he said, getting right to the point. "I should've told you how I really felt about you. I never meant to hurt you."

"Oh, yeah? So, why didn't you tell me?" She cut him a sideways glance. "And why are you suddenly confessing now? Are you worried it's going to come back to bite you somehow?" She stopped abruptly and whirled around. "Are you getting married? Is that it?"

"No," he argued, stunned at her accusation. "Is that what you think of me? A liar and a cheater?"

"You tell *me*. Are you?"

We're getting nowhere fast.

"The truth is, Ava, I'm in a no-win situation. And I'm a fool for not straightening it out when I should have done so."

The massive crowd swarmed past them, moving like a steady current. She folded her arms and began walking again.

"You were dead right about Henry Hamilton and Richard Santorio," he said. "They were very close matches, but there was another one that turned out to be your most *perfect* match."

"What?" She stopped again. "What do you mean

by that?"

Don't blow this opportunity by injecting your opinions. Just stick to the facts...

He took a deep breath. "There was one profile that matched yours right down to the last detail but, because of technicalities, it was thrown out."

"What do you mean?" Her face paled as her eyes widened. "What profile? What technicalities?"

"The profile couldn't be used because...well, because it was mine."

Her mouth fell open in slow motion.

Expecting her to be upset, he continued on in a rush, desperate to make her understand. "Back in the early days of the company, when we were beta testing our profiling system, we didn't have enough people to crossmatch with our test clients, so we added all the profiles of our employees," he added quickly. "When our software developer found out what we'd done, we were told to purge everyone from the database because we were skewing the results. I don't know why, but for some reason, mine was overlooked. We didn't realize it until Dawson drew your matches and mine topped the list."

She didn't say anything, but her blank stare

clearly indicated her level of shock.

"Dawson laughed about it and deleted my profile, but when you rejected Henry Hamilton, it stunned him. Normally, we don't offer our beta testers a second chance for free, but in your case, Dawson felt committed to try again and convinced Richard Santorio, your third match, to take Henry's place."

"Neither one of them were right for me," she said finally, "and when I complained a second time, he sent *you,* of all people, to clean up the mess. Didn't he realize what a heavy risk he was taking?"

Jeff shoved his hands into his pockets. "I think he figured that since I was your closest match, I would be the best candidate to approach you because I could relate to you." He stared down at the floor, taking a much-needed moment to prepare for what he was about to reveal. "He had no way to know that I would fall in love with you." He looked up. "Neither did I."

Her face turned scarlet. "You mean to tell me you left the island without telling me how you felt about me?"

Jeff pulled her close, not caring if hundreds of people *were* staring at them. "Ava, when Dawson hired me, I signed a confidentiality agreement with respect to profile information and a conflict of interest agreement, attesting in writing that I'd never get romantically involved with any Perfect Match client. By the time I left the island, I'd convinced myself I was simply infatuated with you and that it would pass, but it didn't, and one day I finally admitted to myself what I'd been denying all along. I was miserable without you."

She looked up, tears in her eyes. "Is that why you got Lisa to trick me into coming to the open house? Why didn't you just call me and be honest with me?"

"A few weeks after I got back, I saw Amy and asked her about you. She said you'd gotten a new job and you were really happy. It sounded to me like you'd forgotten all about me. So, I let it go."

A group of middle-school boys passed by, making kissing noises and laughing. One boy yelled, "Hey, get a room!"

Jeff let her go and took her hand in his. "Come on, let's find someplace private to talk."

"You didn't answer my question," Ava said as they moved along past store after store. "Why did you use Lisa to get me to come to the open house?"

"I didn't," he answered honestly. "Dawson is to blame for that. When I showed up at the Miami office, all gloomy and depressed, he must have figured it out. He told Amy and she told Lisa. The three of them conspired together. He admitted as much the moment you and Lisa showed up." Jeff laughed wryly. "He hinted that I'd been moping for three months and it was now or never for me to straighten things out with you."

They reached a corner and turned to their right, walking past a teen clothing store. The floor under their feet literally vibrated from the loud music emanating from the shop. They kept walking past more clothing boutiques, shoe stores and a designer handbag store. Nearing the rotunda, they passed a cookie shop and a large candy store. Jeff casually glanced through the opening of the candy store as they approached and did a double take. He tugged at Ava's hand. "Come on."

He led her to an instant photo booth for couples called "Sweetheart Shots." Parting the curtains, he ducked his head and slid into the booth, pulling Ava after him. Once she sat down beside him, he reached over and drew the curtains shut.

Ava glanced around. "No one would ever believe me if I told them I'd squeezed into a photo booth with you in a candy store for a heart-to-heart talk."

He smiled. "I kid you not. This is probably the

only place where we'll have complete privacy in this entire mall, but it won't be for long so I have to talk fast." He slid his hand under her chin and turned her face toward his. No more delays. "I love you, Ava. I've loved you since the day I kissed you at Turquoise Cove."

"Deep down, I realized it, too, and it didn't make any sense to me why you wouldn't tell me. That's why I ran away from you in the parking lot." Her eyes softened as her gaze melded with his. "I knew something had changed between us, but I didn't think it had affected you the way it did me so it was easier to pretend it never happened." She slid her hands under the lapels of his jacket. "In my heart, I couldn't deny you were my perfect match. And so, I fell in love with you, too."

Cupping her face in his hands, he pulled her close and kissed her passionately, determined to make up for lost time and to let his actions prove he'd never back away from her *ever* again.

A group of pre-teens had gathered outside the booth, laughing and shoving each other around as they waited their turn. "What are they doing in there," one girl announced loudly. "They've been in there a *long* time." The group began to giggle.

"Don't they know they have to put money in the

machine to get their pictures?"

"They've probably never been in one before. They're kinda *old*..."

More giggling.

"Hey, you guys," one of the girls shouted over their horseplay. "Can you hurry up and pay so we can get our turn?

Annoyed, Jeff reluctantly pulled away and shoved his fist into his pocket. He pulled out a five-dollar bill and thrust his hand past the curtain. "Is this enough?"

More giggling. Someone took the money from his hand and fed it into the machine.

He grinned at Ava. "Get ready. We're going to be on camera any moment now."

She slid her hands around his neck and lifted her chin, meeting him halfway. He angled his head and closed his eyes as he kissed her passionately, not caring when or how the pictures snapped. He just wanted to show her how much he loved her.

Chapter Fifteen

March 19th- Enchanted Island

The Perfect Match

THE BRIGHT SPRING sun shone down relentlessly, reflecting off the crystal waves of the Caribbean Sea as Ava and Jeff sat on the deck of the parasail vessel in their swing-like harnesses, waiting for the "go-ahead" from the captain. The red and white parasail wing, fully open, floated behind them, catching the wind as the boat glided toward the open sea.

Though it was the first time she'd ever tried parasailing, she felt no fear whatsoever, only calm delight and the expectation of an exciting ride.

Jeff reached out and squeezed her knee. "Are you okay?"

She nodded.

"Are you sure? You're so quiet. We don't have to

go through with it if you don't want to."

She smiled. "I'm not afraid. I'm looking forward to it."

At her urging, he'd let his hair grow again and the thick, blond curls he'd had last time they'd stayed on the island were starting to grow back. That was the Jeff she fell in love with—a happy, carefree "surfer dude." She never wanted that aspect of him to change. Or his love of adventure.

The captain stepped to the back of the boat. "Are you ready?"

"Yes," they said in unison.

"All right, let's go." He turned and signaled to the driver. The boat sped up, the winch on the tow rope released and the wind slowly lifted Ava and Jeff, flying tandem, into the air. Higher and higher they climbed until the water became a mass of aqua as far as her eyes could see. Below her, the boat's foamy white wake cut a path through the tranquil surface of the vast sea.

The farther they climbed, the more relaxing and serene the atmosphere became. Ava took a deep breath and smiled to herself. Ten months ago, on this day, she was packing her suitcase to fly to West Palm Beach and attend Lisa's baby shower. Little did she know how much that event would change her life, how much it would eventually change *her*.

After they returned from this trip, they were going to start shopping for an engagement ring. No wedding date would be set for a while, but they'd already decided the honeymoon would be a much grander affair than the nuptials. Then they would find the right house, get a puppy and have a baby or two.

But for now, she was content to let her feet dangle high above the sea and just enjoy the beauty of being alive. And sharing that life with the man she loved.

Jeff leaned toward her and slid his hand around the base of her neck, drawing her closer. "I love you!" he shouted in the wind.

She laughed. "I love you!"

"I'm the luckiest man in the world!" He drew her face close to his and kissed her. "We're going to have a great life together."

They'd only just begun.

The End

Author Bio

Denise Devine is a USA TODAY bestselling author of sweet contemporary romance who has had a passion for books since the second grade when she discovered Little House on the Prairie by Laura Ingalls Wilder. She wrote her first book, a mystery, at age thirteen and has been writing ever since. If you'd like to know more about her, you can visit her website at www.deniseannettedevine.com.

PERFECT MATCH THANKS YOU

Thanks for reading Ava's story! Maeve's book is next. You'll find a Sneak Peek in the Excerpt.

Find all the Perfect Match books at Amazon!
BREE (Raine English)
MARNI (Aileen Fish)
MOLLY (Julie Jarnagin)
JADE (Rachelle Ayala)
AVA (Denise Devine)
MAEVE (Josie Riviera)

For more fun and romance, be sure to read the Beach Brides series, the inspiration for Perfect Match. It involves twelve friends who decide to meet on a Caribbean island. As a silly dare during her last night there, each heroine decides to stuff a note in a bottle addressed to her "dream hero" and cast it out to sea.

Find the Beach Brides at Amazon!
https://www.amazon.com/Beach-Brides/e/B071HW8F9H

Excerpt Copyright Information, Prologue and Chapter One from Maeve (Perfect Match Series) by Josie Riviera. Copyright © 2018 Josie Riviera

Maeve

Perfect Match Series

By

Josie Riviera

Prologue

Maeve's Perfect Matching Dating Profile ...

Miss Irish Independence, Age 26

"When he takes me in his arms, he speaks to me softly, I see the world through rose-colored glasses."— Edith Piaf, French singer, songwriter, and film actress.

I live for a hot cuppa tea and will share it with you.

I'm a good listener. But make no mistake, I follow my own dreams, not yours.

Love comes in many forms, and I believe in a commitment to one person.

Be warned ... I'm a workaholic.

CHAPTER ONE

"IT'LL DO YOU good to get away from Ireland. We've had a rainy summer."

"Rainy summer?" Maeve Doherty grinned at her best friend, Colleen O'Keefe, who was busily swiping Maeve's phone. "When can you recall a non-wet summer in Ireland?"

"A year ago. It was on a Thursday."

Maeve laughed out loud. As always, her flaming-haired friend's sunny disposition lifted her spirits.

Colleen chuckled in return. Her tailored canary-yellow pantsuit, with matching pumps, fit her full-figured body impeccably. Maeve glanced at her own worn linen skirt and smoothed her wrinkled polyester blouse. When had she last taken time for herself? She'd forgotten, it had been so long ago, with all the worry and sleepless nights.

Colleen plunked into an oversized chair in the lobby of the building that housed the Merrimac Company. The women were purchasing agents for a small Irish hotel chain. Their duties included placing orders for everything from hotel furniture to cleaning supplies and comparing various prices and the quality of the merchandise.

Colleen pointed with one of her French manicured fingernails at Maeve's phone screen. "If I'm reading this email correctly, you've been offered a free week at the paradise island of your choice, compliments of the Perfect Match dating agency."

Maeve pulled up a chair across from her friend. "Aye."

Keeping her fingertip on the blinking cursor, Colleen paused. "You plan to accept, don't you?"

"Whatever the catch is, it's not worth a week anywhere on the globe."

"This offer is from Amy Yates, your friend from America, and her husband, Dawson. It's a personalized invitation." Colleen scanned Maeve's phone screen. "A free vacation, a romantic getaway, a chance—"

Maeve held up a hand. "Aye."

"So, it's legit," Colleen declared gaily. "I remember you said they owned the agency."

"Aye."

"Which island are you choosing?"

"I'm not choosing any island because I'm not going."

"How about Corsica, France?" Colleen obviously pretended she hadn't heard Maeve. "You've always wanted to learn French. And isn't there a famous museum there you've always wanted to visit?"

"Maison Bonaparte, the ancestral home of the Bonaparte family." Maeve nodded. "The museum is located in Ajaccio, Corsica."

"Then go."

"Yes, someday, on my own, using my own money—not obligated to a matchmaking agency."

Colleen pushed her glasses up her nose and peered at the phone. "All expenses are paid and the terms and conditions are clearly spelled out. All you have to do is agree to spend the week with your match or risk being charged for the vacation."

Maeve lifted a skeptical eyebrow. "That's all?"

"It's a massive marketing campaign to introduce their new business," Colleen reminded her. "You're helping them as much as they're helping you."

"I love history, but I'm not that desperate to see Napoléon Bonaparte's death mask. I'd prefer spending a cozy week in my flat reading a pile of European history books." Maeve tapped her fingers together and drew in a breath. "Figure in a hot cuppa Irish tea and lemon scones from The Ground Café and I'll be merry as a leprechaun."

"You're emotionally spent," her friend said quietly. "And you gave Amy Yates permission to plug your name into the Perfect Match database."

Maeve turned a despairing look on Colleen. "Aye, in a flash of desperation when I feared any opportunity for love was passing me by. I'm over that."

Was she?

Once she'd recovered from the sadness and shock of learning her twenty-year-old brother Owen had been diagnosed with cancer, she'd settled into the daily task of tending to him when he opted to move in with her rather than live with their mother. She'd given up every pastime she enjoyed to care for him, including auditioning for minor acting roles, something she loved.

Now that Owen's radiation treatments were over and his caregiving routine had become stable, perhaps she could ease up a bit, take a breather. Perhaps...

"Maeve?" Colleen prodded. "Owen is in remission and he can go live with your mother for a week. She's able-bodied and can tend to him. You're only twenty-six. Live your life."

"Most days my mother isn't capable of washing a dish, let alone attending to a sick adult. She had a hard-enough time being a parent when Owen was well."

"Your mother lands in the middle of drama because of the type of men she sees, and her ongoing dilemmas can't always be your problem." Colleen leaned back in her chair. Her normally keen bright-blue gaze softened. "Enough about your mother. What's the craic with you? Are you sleeping okay?"

Maeve shrugged. "I'm always tired, although everyone is exhausted nowadays because of our hectic lifestyles."

"Grab this chance. Go. Believe me, if it weren't for my boyfriend, Colin, I'd take your place."

Colleen and Colin had an on-again, off-again

relationship that had lasted for over a year. Currently, it was on again.

A reassuring grin crossed Colleen's freckled face. "Along with Owen's healthcare providers, your mother will mind him brilliantly. I want to see an optimistic smile on your face again. I'm sure you'll have a lorry-load of stories to share when you get back."

Maeve shook her head. "Because of all the days I missed when Owen became ill, I'm on the verge of losing my job. I certainly can't afford to take off any more time. Besides, his medical bills are mounting, and our private insurance only covers part of them."

"You're physically and mentally exhausted. *Your* health is important too. You need the time away to maintain your sense of balance."

"Aye, perhaps," Maeve admitted. Her brother's cancer journey had been a lengthy road crowded with difficult decisions and the challenges of radiation treatment.

"The Merrimac Company wants to branch out of Ireland and explore resort areas for other hotels. Pitch the idea to our manager. Tell Mrs. McShea it's a working holiday. Just think you'll get paid for sitting on a beach in a bikini."

"I don't swim, and I've never worn a bikini."

"Live a wee bit, Maeve. Spend your days lying in a lounge chair and looking out at the Mediterranean. You once told me there are over two hundred beaches in Corsica. Imagine the sun, the surf—"

"Colleen—"

"The sand." Colleen laughed. "It's a win-win. Besides, who can pass up the chance to meet Mr. Right?"

"I'm too busy to fritter away my valuable time on a man. And there's no such man as Mr. Right, at least not for me."

"How do you know? Make the time."

"Suppose he's not interesting?"

"Suppose he is?"

"What about Crinkles?"

"Your dog is accustomed to your ma's flat." Colleen tapped the phone screen again. Amy says her agency's matchmaking algorithms are the best and they're launching this campaign to prove it."

"And if you keep scrolling, you'll see they want people who've been unlucky in love."

Like her.

Maeve studied Merrimac's lobby—a gleaming brown floor, mahogany table, anything but her friend's sympathetic stare. She'd spilled out more than she'd intended.

A year ago, while visiting a cousin in America, she'd met Amy while shopping in an exclusive boutique, not realizing at first that she was chatting with the owner of the boutique. They'd become instant friends, and they shared coffee and heartfelt conversation after the store closed. That evening, Maeve had poured out her sadness to her new-found confidante.

Finbar, Maeve's boyfriend of two years, had broken up with her—not even in person—but through a dismissive text.

"No more," she'd declared to Amy. "Men and their hollow promises are not to be believed."

Wasn't Maeve's father, who'd left her mother without an explanation, further proof of her statement? He'd said he'd return. He never had.

"Maeve? Maeve?" Colleen yanked Maeve from her upsetting remembrances. "I'm partial to the final line of your dating profile." She read aloud: "'Love comes in many forms, and I believe in a commitment to one person.' Colleen looked up at Maeve. "Aww, that's very sweet. You expressed yourself perfectly."

Heat rose in Maeve's face. "I'm starry-eyed and foolish for writing something so reckless. No one stays with one person forever."

"Some do. Some people have a love that lasts. Where are those rose-colored glasses you used to wear?"

"I've put them away and become realistic."

"Dust them off. What if Mr. Right is waiting for you in Corsica?"

"He won't be, although just to be sure ..." Maeve grabbed her phone from Colleen and included another line at the bottom of her dating profile.

Be warned ... I'm a workaholic.

Colleen squinted at the screen. "Being a workaholic is supposed to deter him?"

"I'll plead nine-to-five obligations."

Plus, any other excuses necessary to safeguard her heart.

"So, it's settled." Colleen flashed a quick smile. "You'll accept Amy's offer and choose Corsica."

"Aye." Maeve feigned enthusiasm, then blew out a breath.

She'd go, she'd rest, she'd work. But she wouldn't risk falling in love.

Once was enough. Besides, if there was a perfect match for her on God's emerald-green planet, she'd have found him by now in Ireland.

"That's grand," Colleen said. "Finally, you're doing something for yourself." With a flourish, Colleen stood and walked over to Maeve, throwing her arms around her. "Get ready, my dear friend, for an amazing adventure!"

*** End of excerpt***

Maeve (Perfect Match Series) by Josie Riviera

Made in the USA
Lexington, KY
31 May 2018